Chapter 1.
Introduction.

1982 The day of yet another meeting.

Nick had been employed by the 'Yorkshire Post' since
he had left school at the age of sixteen, starting as a
deputy reporter in 1977. He was a bright lad, usually
wearing a shirt and tie, although he preferred not to
wear a suit. His hair clean, fashionably long, and untidy
if not a tad wild, framing his large nose that may have
been happier supporting, or at least hiding behind a pair
of glasses. He was always in the centre of the action,
full of fun, cracking jokes and pulling others' legs. With
a sparkle 'n' glint in his eye which the girls loved and
made the boys wary, he was a little rebellious and always up to some mischief.

Although the editor was not to too keen, he came to
work in all weathers on his GPZ550 Kawasaki motorcycle. On this particular day he had been called in by
his superior and his heart had sank. The U.K. was in a
bit of a pickle with riots and strikes being common-
place. He feared the worst - being laid off or placed
onto a one or two day week, as few colleagues had
been. At best maybe sent on a fact finding mission on
some crazy dog like Arthur Scargill, leader of the
Miners Union.

Nick had made sure he was up earlier than normal, trying to get some breakfast down his throat. He placed a
bowel on the kitchen table and moved toward the cereal
cupboard. He started to open the cupboard door and
slowly closed it again. Realising he was too worried to
eat, he left the kitchen and went to his bedroom to dress
and be at his best for the meeting with his boss.

1

Unusually he did his top button up, tied his tie with a Windsor knot and wore the jacket matching his suit trousers, which he had just pulled the rear tails down to. He forgot about the oil under his fingernails and was now knocking on the editor's door. Once the formalities and hand shaking was over, his editor smiled. He was clean shaven, dark hair slicked back with some stinking lotion or potion. He wore thick dark framed glasses to support his sight. He was a man who knew what he wanted, and his enthusiasm was not going to get in his way. He congratulated Nick on his diligent work to date. This was a bit of a surprise and Nick started to feel a little lighter inside as he was being given his first ever one on one assignment.

He was instructed to go and meet with a character by the name of 'Murtyl' - an acquaintance of 'Bill' the editor. This Murtyl person was expecting him to arrive this Sunday morning at around 1100hrs. Nick was just about to protest and then thought better of it, remembering all those employees who were being placed on short time etc. It was, well, bloody test Saturday and race Sunday. He was supposed to be testing his TZ and not going to work. Hutton Rudby - he knew roughly where it was, and now had the full address from Bill. He thanked Bill for the opportunity as he turned away and exited Bill's office. On the bright side it was his first ever real job he had been assigned to for the paper. On the rubbish side, he was now going to have to tell his mates he had to work. Saturday was going to be prepping questions, washing and ironing. Sunday, well he was just going to have to catch up with them on the evening and see how they had got on. His feet became heavy as he moved towards the exit and his legs leaden with a lack of enthusiasm to propel him forward, or for that matter, keep him upright. He really dreamt of riding, being best of the late brakers, smoothest round the corners and first on the throttle driving out of the

2

corner, gaining better traction and drive than his rivals (rather than having the best and quickest blurry fingers over a QUERTY board), hitting the shift and sliding back the roll better than anyone else. The ideal was to be first over the finish line, with a comfortable lead, on the back wheel, with one hand in the air while the crowd roared in appreciation. Nick understood track time was the only way to improve. He was not sure if he was good enough, but he did know that he did not have the kind of money required to make it all a little easier. So Sunday, he had better show an enthusiastic face, as without the job, things would be a whole lot tougher than they were at present.

Saturday had been booked as a test day at the local race circuit, distance wise that was a toss-up between Oulton Park and Croft Autodrome. He had been brought up in Teesside and so in his mind Croft was his local. Nick had been looking forward to getting home that evening and going through his final preparations for Saturday's test. Although his bike was second hand, it was a completely new beast to him. A Yamaha TZ 250cc G, originally purchased by Armstrong Motorcycles. Their semi-professional rider Alan Taylor had won the British 250cc championship on it five years earlier. Nick had done well to get it out of Armstrong and Russ the owner, with all the tuning parts still on it. The BMW and Honda dealership did not need to let the bike go to any Tom, Dick, or Harry. Without the influence of Dave and Will Hardy of Hardy Bros garage, Saltwells Road, Middlesbrough, he would have stood no chance of acquiring such a strong contender with his finances. Dave Hardy in his day had been 'Cock of the North' and a well-respected racer, while a mechanic who worked with them, John Webb or "Webby" had also been 'Cock of the North' by winning at Oliver's Mount in Scarborough. He had also run well in the British Championships, to the degree he had been requested to compete

3

for the U.K. against the U.S.A in the Transatlantic series. With these guys on his side, surely they were going to be a formidable team, he hoped…

His spirits had lifted momentarily as these things ran through his mind, and then he was back down to earth, knowing all the planning for the weekend had just been kicked in the nuts and was now out of the window. He knew he was going to miss all the action at the track and have to wait until Sunday evening to hear about all his mates' heroics and blunders, after he returned from visiting this Murtyl character. By heck, it better be good stuff he was going to get from this visit, as he was pretty miffed about missing the weekend he had planned and prepared so long for!

He needed to get home and prepare for Sunday. In his heart he knew Bill would not have given him this on a weekend unless he thought there was something in it. So, with this in mind, his enthusiasm and hopes began to rise again, even if only a little.

Sunday morning came soon enough, his questions and note pad at the ready, a new Bic Stilo or Biro at the ready, and his best suit on. On top of this he placed his 'Barbour' wax cotton jacket, with pants guaranteeing as far as possible, him staying dry on the road if the heavens opened. These, as well as his boots, were old and out of vogue, however they were functional, and it left him with a little spare monies for his race kit. He was earning £21.00 per week and things were rather hand to mouth. Doing without was fine, as long as he got out and raced the TZ as best he could. As long as the rent, electricity, water etc was paid at the end of the quarter, he did not care about anything but getting out and racing.

Nick removed all the locks and chains after checking the oil and fuel levels on his little Kawasaki and then lubed the chain. Placing the key in the ignition, he turned it on. Then he pulled out the choke and pressed the starter button once - the kill switch had been placed into the run position. The old suck, squeeze, bang, blow system of the four stroke four cylinder machine worked a treat, firing into life as the second or third piston went up on its compression stroke. These Japanese bikes were just a tad more reliable than the fading British ones. He slowly warmed the engine up blipping her between 1000rpm and 2500rpm while releasing the choke.

He had planned a route that offered the most fun rather than be the most direct. There was no fun in riding in straight lines. The fun on a bike was to be had during, pre and post corners. Looking for the apex and getting it just right, was the challenge. Of course, on the road rather than the track there were other things to think about - cyclists, cars parked just around blind bends, farmers spreading muck over the road and those deadly diesel leaks and spills. These all added to entertainment and let's face it, risk is entertainment in all its forms, whether it's your life that's on the line, your hard earned cash or your honour.

Nick beared left off the A19 heading North onto the A172, he clover- leafed around to the right, passed the Tontine hotel and restaurant, and then beared left again off towards Stokesley. The long sweeping right hander that took you back over the A19, was one of those corners you really needed to keep your wits about you. It craved you to sweep into the right of the road to take the best line. However, the signage never seemed to mention this stretch was two way. Poor Davy Rudd (a friend) had found that out the hard way and ended up in the Friarage Hospital for months, recovering from spinal injuries. The car driver hadn't even bothered to stop. (There are words for those sorts) Nick remembered just as he was naturally about to peel into that part of the road. He carried on along the A172 for a few miles until he came to the Potto turn off to the left. This was a better stretch of slick little bends and he enthusiastically went up and down through the gear box, keeping the revs at their most efficient. While using the brakes front and rear he slowed and controlled the bike to get the best out of her. Occasionally, he scraped the foot pegs and centre stand on the road, but this was just making it all the more enjoyable.

Approaching a T- junction he slowed, indicated to the right, and looked left, right, left again before proceeding on towards his destination. Braking for the thirty 30 mph signs, he entered the village of Hutton Rudby. He passed some relatively new properties on either side and then some terraced houses, one being a pub called The Station. A little further on he reached the summit of a brow - there was a funeral directors on the left. Just as his mind was wandering to the death department of life, his eyes caught the brilliance the village green, it was beautiful. He followed the first tributary road to the left up past the Green Grocers and then the Spa shop. Further up he could see a butchers and the Kings Head pub - another terrace house converted into an ale house. He was beginning to think it could a great place to live. He now turned to the right and back down the hill to the other end of the village, noting the great oak and chestnut trees on the green. What a place, and at the end of that there were two more pubs The Wheatsheaf Inn and the Bay Horse. He parked his ride in the Bay's car park and removed his helmet, then carried all his stuff to the wall to arrange his kit and get the wax cottons off. Looking around, he could see that the Wheat was on 'East Side', so he glanced up and down the cottages.

6

Yes, there she was, three doors down from the Wheatsheaf, where he was going to meet with Murtyl.

'Green View' was written on a plaque next to the front door. What a bonus not to walk around asking where it might be. Now prepped and ready it was 5 mins to the hour – a little early but that's fine, much better than being late and disrespectful. He wrapped his knuckle several times against the front door, but received no response. Saddened he walked around to see where he may find the rear door. An enclosed driveway led him to the old coach route down by the side of the Wheatsheaf where the stables used to be a hundred or so years ago. Here he saw a beautiful 1969 Triumph Tr 6 650. The parallel twin was in prime condition and he was quite surprised at the styling of her. All the standard kit was as it should be, right hand gear change, twin leading front shoe front brake and quick release rear wheel. In fact, exactly what the legendary Steve McQueen had ridden in the SDT in East Germany during 1968. However, there were a few extras – cow horn American style handlebars making her a little lighter to steer, a Siamese town into one up and over exhaust, pearlised black and white painted tank, by she was stunning.

Just as he was getting carried away in a daydream state again, he remembered why he was there. Looking around he saw the Kitchen door of the Wheatsheaf pub was open, releasing the heat on such a busy day for lunch. Knocking on the old open door, he asked if anyone knew of a person called Murtyl and where he may find them. The answer came back sharp from the clearly over worked chef. "T'other side of that ruddy Triumph over there, in the garage I bet!" Nick thanked him for his help and wandered off, crossed the courtyard or beer garden area.

7

He quickly spotted a pair of legs sticking out from under the front of and old light metallic blue Austin Healy. The chrome blinged and she (the car) was stunning. The legs from under her were drab to say the least. Oily work boots were hiding small feet and the legs were covered by those fifties style light brown cotton overalls or boiler suit. The back of the car was up on ramps and the front was on axle stands allowing good safe access to her underneath. Her front wheels were off, and Nick could see the brake drums were not standard cast rusty things. They were blued by excessive heat and were definitely after-market. The brake hoses were braided with steel wire to stop brake fade, caused by high temperatures. Nick was bloody well intrigued at the thought of this but reminded himself to get cracked on with the job at hand, so he took a deep breath and asked. "Excuse me Sir, I am looking for a Mr Murtyl. My name is Nick and I believe you are expecting me!"

A sharp dry Yorkshire response quickly came back. "You'll find no ruddy Mr Murtyl here lad!" then nothing. Nick waited as the legs in the brown coveralls started to slide out from under the car. Then in one sweeping movement one oily hand appeared to grip the car's bumper after lofting a few rags over the chrome. The hips and torso seemed to glide out effortlessly, then a slight roll to the side and the shoulders and head which all followed in one fluid motion. As the body stood prior to turning Nick noticed how small the man was and narrow at the waist. Just as his eyes were stumbling around the man wearing a red polka dot bandana, the entity turned to face him. Then it hit him. He was a blinkin' girl, or lady or whatever, in a man's boiler suit, working on a car! The lady person looked Nick up and down as if assessing him and then asked, "Biker, are you lad?"

Nick replied in a rather surprised manner, "Yess ma'am." Then carried on keeping the conversation going. "Well yes I suppose so, been riding trials since I was thirteen and have been doing Saturdays to help out where I can at the 'Hardy Bros' down at Saltwells Road in Middlesbrough."

The woman smiled a broad happy smile and asked, "Know 'Will n Dave' do you? Must have a way to go though as I've not heard of no, up and coming local Lampkin or Mick Grant." He was taken back a little. She knew people he did and yet he had never heard or seen her before. If nothing else, he would have remembered the Triumph and Healy, if he had seen them before. Nick doubted this was Murtyl, for no particular reason other than he was a she, or she was a he in his mind for some reason, if you know what I mean.

She then started to release words from her mouth again and interrupted his incoherent rambling. "Nick's your name, yes?" As she thrust out her oily hand to shake his, she carried on with,

"Shake lad, pleased to meet you, never mind the oil, and yes, I am Murtyl, the one you're looking for." His hand went out to meet the hand of a lady ready for the soft and gentle touch of a woman. His hand was actually met by a small, gentle, well-manicured hand that happened to still be oily after being wiped with rags. The slippery grip expected was a little different to what he actually received, which was at first momentarily firm, quickly rising to crushing painful grip, and just as quickly faded back into the gentle touch of a lady. Nick almost tried to tear his hand away and would have, if the whole motion had not been so devastatingly fast. She turned and motioned him to follow as she walked toward the rear door of her home. He followed obediently, observing the sway of her hips, the narrow waist and clean line of her shoulders. He estimated she was between 5ft 4in to 5ft 6in in height. The bandana hid all her hair and he had noticed there had been no makeup. At the door, the boots were flicked off and she bade him to do the same before walking into the cottage. Once in, he followed her to the kitchen where she first washed her hands in Swafega and then in Fairy washing up liquid. After drying her hands, she instructed him to do the same while asking him to make a pot of tea and pointing to where things were, she then removed the bandana. Her lightly curled hair cascaded or rolled down to her shoulders, framing the cheerful, pretty, roundish face. As she left the kitchen, he was advised to use the china cups and she would return in just a few minutes. Nick was on the case and wasted no time in making the tea, placing the china cups and saucers on a tray with the tea pot and taking them into the dining room where he placed the tray on the dining table. Well-mannered as ever, he did not take a seat, but mused at the pictures on the wall.

There were pictures of this lady and trophies all over. The pictures were at different racing tracks with cars that she possibly had driven, and others of her with some of the greats. Moss, Fangio, Hill, Clark and more. He was thinking she must have travelled a bit and been around the world just by the fact that some of these photographs were from European, American, and South American tracks. There were also images of her with road racers and scramblers too. Mesmerized by what he was seeing, he realised he had been lucky to have been sent to interview a person who would seem to have lived his passion: danger, risk, hot engines, fast cars and bikes. A few minutes had gone by and as he turned to the third wall where the stairs were, he looked up, just at the right time to see this lady descend into the room. No shoes, but calves to die for started to glide effortlessly down. Followed by a tight but not too tight pencil-y (he thought) skirt which rounded over the hips nestling into that narrow waist. Out of the top of that skirt came a cream to white blouse, buttoned up to one or two below the collar. The bosom was there but his eye flew straight by to the eyes, crystal clear, penetrating ice blue which he nearly fell into. The nose was sharp and defined but in his mind's eye, simply perfect. The lips were full, with a little silky red colour on them. His face must have given him away.

The lady stopped descending with one or two steps to go and smiled, "I saw the twinkle in your eye Nick, it is very kind of you to let an old lady feel a little younger. I have spent quite a while choosing the correct person to follow this through. Everybody I have spoken to or asked who knows you, have told me you can be trusted to complete a task in the manner to be agreed. Is this correct?" Then she carried on down the last two steps and took a seat at the dining table. Before he could answer, she carried on with, "They say I can trust you, that you work hard and you're honest, which is good. In my case I will be the judge, and you will have to win my trust. Just so you know, I do know a bad one when I see one and have dispatched a few in my time!" Nick's mind raced, she had obviously done her homework and knew enough about him to embarrass his knowledge of her - some bloody reporter he was! All he could come up with was, "Ma am, all I know is how to be me. I do my best to be the 'Best of the Best' in everything I do. Oddly, I have lived like that for as long as I can remember."
She replied. "I know you do Nick; I'm not accusing you of anything, just stating fact. I have known Bill for a long time, he knows I have travelled and realises as a reporter, there maybe something of interest in my past. He has seen the same things you have and has asked several times. The answer was always the same, there is a story, but it will only be given when I choose and to whom I choose at a time of my choosing." Nick's mind still raced as to what this could all be about as she started to speak again. "Right Nick, first things first. You have called me Ma-am too often already, you call me

'Murtyl'- nothing else. Not Miss Murtyl, Mrs Murtyl or Mr Murtyl, just bloody Murtyl O.K.?" Nick nodded in acknowledgment as more came out. "It's a Sunday and you should be out having fun. The weather is fine so get off with you and come back here at 1100hrs sharp a week on Friday."

Nick answered immediately with, "Yes Sir!" as his up-bringing had conditioned him to where hearing the twenty four hour clock being used.

She immediately reprimanded him, "I just stated it's 'Murtyl' and only that!"

He quickly corrected himself and carried on. "I'm here now and all my mates are at the track. You're on with that Healy and I could give you a hand." Then weakly added, "What with the nights getting longer and things, I can help…" Murtyl smiled in a way that oozed satis-faction, confidence and just that something else, that thing you can't put your finger on, and there is no Eng-lish word for it. Maybe not, that smile was just 'IT'- that indefinable something that is very very special. She then ordered, "Put the overalls on that are hanging in the garage and I will be back down ready to start in a few minutes." As she rose and climbed up the stairs, Nick smiled to himself and thought bloody hell, she's great! He made his way to the open garage and put on the overalls that were hanging by the door, after taking his suit jacket off and trousers and laying them over a dining room chair with his tie.

Chapter 2.
Gear Box, Dirt n Grime with a bit of language.

The first thing noticed as he moved into position under Murtyl's Healy was the prop-shaft had been removed and all the relevant cables had been disconnected. These were held to one side neatly with small bits of wire, each being labelled as to its use and adjustment. 'Very tidy' he thought to himself. Together they removed the gear box supports and the clutch bell housing bolts. These bolts were a bit of a sod with not a lot of manoeuvring room or space for your spanner and hand together. Once this was all done, the gearbox and bell housing's weight was supported by a trolley jack as it was levered and pulled away from the rear of the big 2.664 litre straight six engine. Now Nick was in a bit of a conundrum, he just couldn't see a way of getting that gearbox and housing out from under the car. It was not just the space available, there were cross members in the way. Murtyl slid out from under the car on her side and spoke to Nick, "Come on lad, hop to it, there's lots to do before she's lifted!"

Nick was out from under the car quick smart and thought he better mention something. "Excuse me, but can I mention something?"

The reply came abrupt as ever. "Get on with it lad."

"Well Murtyl, I can see the point of lifting the car off the box, but there are cross members stopping that." Nick stated.

Murtyl replied. "Yes Nick, that is correct and in most rear wheel drive cars the box would be dropped. However, in this Healy's case, the box must be lifted through the cabin after the floor & transmissions tunnel have been removed with the seats. Look inside her, you can see they are all out."

Nick looked into the car and saw this was so. He felt a little stupid and realised she really did know what she was doing. He then asked, "So you lift the box etc out of the car and wheel the car away from under it, is that the idea!"

"Yes Nick, that is the tried and proven method of choice." She answered.

"So, you've done this before?" he asked.

Murtyl answered, "Yeeeehhhhs (almost in a questioning way) a few times but not just for fun." She smiled back at him. He watched her fettling a few things before they used the block and tackle attached to the roof. Her hands moved confidently around tools and ropes. No wonder the Hardy Bros and others had taken to her. She really was a dream to be around, bright, cheerful, and obviously very knowledgeable regarding this stuff. The pair lifted the box and hosing right above the 100/6 Healy and they pushed the car away from under it. While doing this, Nick noted the suspension was all very much up rated. There was a great sump guard as you would have on a rally off road vehicle and the exhaust was very much an uprated modernisation. A great super charger was bolted to the front of the engine too. Nick whistled to himself and then asked about all the upgrades. The response was short and direct from her, "My old employer liked to know I could move at a pace if required. You will know more as and when I choose to or decide I can trust you. Ok now, eyes on the prize lad!"

Nick replied instinctively, "Yes Sir." and realised he had fluffed it again.

Murtyl stepped in with, "If you really need the Sir stuff you can use 'Chief', but I do prefer Murtyl as it is my name."

He replied, "Yes Murtyl, it will not happen again!"

The first day in the garage and Nick thought he had learnt a lot about Murtyl in quite a short time, even though they had hardly spoken. He had mainly observed and occasionally helped as instructed. He was however, fascinated by her logical and methodical approach with everything. Once an item was used it was wiped or cleaned and placed its correct place.

Nick saw his editor Bill on the Monday. They had a little chat about the Sunday and Bill agreed to give Nick a little leeway with regard to obtaining Murtyl's story and the coming Friday. Nick would now be with Murtyl, if she agreed, most Friday afternoons. He became good friends with her, and he started to share his secrets with her. They spoke in depth about braking techniques on bikes and in cars, where an apex should and should not be used in the dry or wet, where to find the best grip and drive out of a corner. Nick was happy and feeling rather humbled by the amount of time this lady imparted upon himself. In Nick's opinion, Murtyl was indeed all woman and he had seen her in a skirt etc. Her body and the way she glided across the ground put most, if not all the girls he knew to shame, and yet when she got down to business, she out performed over 90% of the best mechanics and men Nick had ever met. He was passed being intrigued. They carried on with the work on the Healy re-lining the clutch, replacing the thrust bearing and pressure plate. She stripped the gear box in front of his eyes with ease, replacing synchromesh for third gear and rebuilding the box with new seals etc. He had never seen a person do this so quickly, while still being meticulous on measurement and cleanliness. She just seem to flow through the whole job as if it were second nature to strip and rebuild such a mechanical device.

Nick asked, "How do you do this, most people I know have to think about what they're doing, and it seems to just flow out of you!"

She replied, "Systems lad, it comes off, check it, clean it and place it in the order it came off. If you need to draw the position it needs to be in, do so as a reminder for when it goes back together. If the tolerances are all good, rebuild - simple and methodical!" As she did so, gears were rotated to make sure they moved freely on their shafts and high spots were causing Resistance to freedom of movement. To Nick it was like watching a soldier strip and re-build his weapon in the dark - smooth as clockwork. He looked around the garage and noted everything had a place and was in its place. This was not like where he kept his bike, nor any other workshop he could remember being in. Even the in- famous Hardys' had a Saturday afternoon tidy up after the week's works. Not this lady though, he thought. He asked without thinking, "Are you always like this Murtyl?"

Murtyl didn't have a clue as to what he was asking about so she said "What are you mumbling about Nick? You could at least give me a clue!"

Nick laughed. "Sorry I was that engrossed I forgot, I mean, are you always so organised neat and tidy with everything?"

Murtyl looked up from her work and suggested, "Less of the questions, but since you asked nicely, I shall an- swer this one; everything is always put away. It gives privacy and security. Sometimes it is just a good way to be, however in my profession, these kind of things of- ten meant life or death, so it is a good habit to retain even though I have retired."

Nick was unsure what she meant by this, and so just nodded as if he understood. He was sure now that she would explain this in the future and in the meantime, he would ponder it all.

Murtyl now piped up. "Well son, not too bad a day. Other than your few hiccups earlier on, you would seem to be a decent lad. So, get cleaned up and be off with you. It's good riding weather and you may just get home in time before they shut your local drinking house. Mind your promise though. I have ears all over!" Nick wasn't sure if he was being kicked out, sent home, or invited back another day so he asked. "Murtyl, I am pleased to be of some help, and I am

16

sorry for the bungles. Mind I have enjoyed being with
you doing some real stuff!"
She answered. "Go get a damned beer and have one for
me. You are welcome anytime, now go!"
To which he set about getting himself ready for the ride
home.

Chapter 3.
The Deal

A few Fridays had rolled by and Murtyl and Nick had
been together, getting on in the garage and doing the
stuff that needed to be done. Nick really did like and
enjoy being in Murtyl's company. She was very straight
talking and when he did something not quite up to her
standards, she was on him with ruthless authority. He
quickly learnt there definitely was the wrong way to do
something, the correct way to do something and
Murtyl's belt n braces way. In her presence it was always the belt n braces, or as he came to know it, 'The
Murtyl way' of doing things.

Because of Nick's upbringing and his own moral compass, he was known as genuine and was trusted by most
- if not all the people that knew him. He was solid, de-
pendable, and never late. He just hoped that Murtyl had
picked up on that as a fact and not fiction.

The two of them had been working as ever on the old
Healy on one particular Friday afternoon. He was just
wiping down the tools they had used and putting them
in their own designated places, as he day-dreamed of
what she may have in the way of secrets to tell.
There was a clap of thunder, the heavens opened, and
the day light reduced dramatically.
The wet came down hard, bouncing off the ground a
few inches before settling, forming puddles then running away in streams to who knew where. He jumped

at first and thought about the wet sodden ride home with that sinking feeling. Murtyl shouted to him from the back doorway, after dodging the drops she could, on her way to that entrance. "Looks like it'll be hard down for a short while, why not wait it out a bit and have a cup of tea while we see what the heavens have in store?"

Nick replied without thinking, "Oh Murtyl that would be grand thank you!"

She replied, "Don't thank me lad, you know where everything is, you close up and get in and make it while I get freshened up and get changed!"

"Yes Ma'am," he replied and was grateful of the offer to stay dry a little longer. He then thought to himself, Oooops used the Ma'am word, then realised that the cheeky bugger had never intended to make the tea. He chuckled to himself and knew it was just her way, as he closed the garage up.

As he entered her home, she regimentally reminded him, "Boots off, soap in the sink, you know the drill." Then she drifted away, and he could hear her stepping up the stair treads toward the landing and then on to who knew where.

Murtyl arrived back in the dining room as Nick placed the mugs of tea on the table with a few ginger nuts biscuits. The two of them sat and nattered for quite a while about various things including how the Healy had been moving forward rapidly, as his extra pair of hands had speeded the job up. He felt quite chuffed to be receiving a kind of compliment and realised she was beginning to trust him. They discussed many things over an hour of two, but mainly about what they doing to her car and what she had in store for it once the jobs were complete.

In her immaculate and elegant way Murtyl peered out of the window at the heavens above and stated, "Well

18

Nick it would seem the rain is not settling just yet. Are you hungry? We worked well together today, and you could stay for dinner?"

She cooked, they ate, and Nick washed and put the dishes away. During this time, they chatted more about the same subjects. Toward the end of the conversation and in Nick's mind trying to change the subject, he sighed, "Well, I do have to say the old girl is looking quite the part and must be just about ready to go!" Murtyl answered without hesitation, "'Yeeeehhssss." (Again, in that quizzical way), "you will have to take her out for a spin when she is completed." And she smiled that knowing smile.

Nick answered as his face lit up with nervous happy thoughts, "Yes I'd love to." realising she was trusting him with her pride and joy and in his mind her baby. "I will look after her!" he stated with his hand on his heart. She just smiled in her own way.

Nick rose from his seat and looked out of the window. It was lighter now, and the pouring had ceased, but the wet ground still soaked up the light. "I'd better get myself ready and get off home while it seems to be drying." She nodded and he could see as he pulled his bike boots on, then his jacket that she was tired. As he left her home Murtyl stated, "You know Nick I enjoy your company, you are welcome anytime and I do have a fair few things to discuss with you, before I have to leave!"

Nick agreed and felt he was at that point of 'Whatever it is I don't know, I think I am going to get to know shortly. Brilliant!' He replied that he looked forward to it and thanked her for dinner as he prepared his bike to leave. The last thing she said was, "Have a safe journey." As he rode away, he could see her waving on the front doorstep, and he thought about driving her car and whatever could be in store for him in the future.

19

The following Monday in the office Nick was called into Bill's office. The questions he was asked were direct. "How are you getting on? What is she really like? Has she told you anything? and Oh come on I really want to know!" While being quite schoolboy like in manner. .

Nick kind of skirted the question by listing what they had been doing and that they got on well. In fact, he really liked her, and could he have some annual leave as he wanted to surprise her. Bill agreed quickly as in his mind Nick would be doing his job while using holidays up, so he and the 'Post' were winning!

The next morning Nick heated up some tomato soup and poured it into a pre heated large flask. Before setting off to Hutton Rudby, he picked up from his local baker some hot freshly baked crispy bread rolls and packed it all into his rucksack. Then he was off on his bike, relaxed and enjoying the ride. His riding style had changed for the better with the old lady's advice. He was cleaner and his pace had definitely picked up a little without any increased dangers. He was smiling to himself at what he had learned from their conversations, regarding various techniques. Knowing she would be under the Healy or at least in the garage, he headed there first. Sure enough the garage door was open, and her legs were sticking out from under the car. He listened to her work, hearing the odd profanity as spanners were picked up and then placed down again after tightening whatever she was tightening. It was a short while before she realised, she had company but once she did she called out, "Hello, who's there, can I help you?"

"Hi Murtyl, its Nick," he answered.

"It's not Friday already is it?" she questioned.

"No Murtyl, its Tuesday. I had some annual leave to use, so I thought I would take you up on your offer of that drive. (His face was getting a little redder as he spoke) Of course only if the offer is still open and she's ready." He was just now realising how cheeky he was being, and his sensitive side was quickly gathering him up into a state of embarrassment.

Murtyl in her overalls slid gracefully out from under the car in that way that only she could.

Holding out her hand to shake his, still covered in oil she spoke, "Lovely to see you, I never break my word and to be honest I wasn't going to run her up without you!" He grinned to the point of the corner of his lips were pushing his ears further round toward the back of his head. She then carried on with, "Of course you'll stay over at least until Friday and we can get on with the job in hand!"

His excitement grew and he replied. "I hoped you would be happy with the idea, so I packed a few things just in case, including some soup and rolls for lunch!"

"That's fine with me lad, let's have an early lunch and see if we can get the old beast struck up this afternoon." she replied. (While knowing Nick would be all over it like hot treacle on a sponge pudding.) They had lunch quick smart and Nick was into his overalls before he washed the dishes. Murtyl allowed this but did warn him it would never do and would not happen again. He wanted to know what they were on with today. Briefly he was told, and they got on with each task; new cables, brakes adjusted, radiator filled, and oil levels checked. After wiping her hands with and an oily rag, she looked him up and down slowly, almost as if inspecting yet, no maybe just checking him over as wise people do. Her right hand went into her overall pocket and quick as a flash reappeared while launching and object for Nick to catch. He did so and looked at her in surprise, "What's this?" he quizzed.

"Oily rag lad, wash up, keys are inside the rag, you can strike her up!" she stated.

"Really - me strike her up?" he quizzed in return.

"Yes Nick, clean yourself, get in, sit down, shut up n belt up. Insert and turn the key to 'ignition on' and I will tell you when to push her starter button. She's fully choked already." Murtyl instructed. Nick obediently followed the instructions to the letter. When Murtyl stuck her thumb up for Nick to see, he knew it was time. The Lucas fuel pump had stopped ticking so he knew her float bowels must be full. He pushed the rubber button on the dashboard. The big six slowly lumbered over a few times and then struck up evenly. The tone Nick could hear from the exhaust was even and mellow like a tenor saxophone when blown exactly right. He looked at the oil pressure and it was good. Murtyl pushed the choke home a little and the idle dropped from 1800 to 1200 rpm. For three or four minutes Murtyl was all over that engine bay looking for leaks and drips. There were none. She then placed the choke into the fully off position and asked Nick to blip the throttle taking her from 800 to 1200 rpm regularly until she was up to normal running temperatures. All the time she moved around the car with stealth and attention which intrigued Nick. It was almost as if she were dancing around the car with joy, while being purposeful.

Leaving the car running, they both returned to the cottage and de oiled themselves.
Once outside again Nick looked less excited and more sheepish in Murtyl's eyes. She asked why he was sat in passenger seat. He made his excuses, "I'm sorry Murtyl, driving this beast on the open road is one thing, but trying to get her out of here, well I just don't want to make a mistake." he uttered.
"Brave lad - know your limits, very sensible, I'll pull her out and you close the door and hop in." she answered. He did so. He looked at the temperature gauge as he sat in the leather seat. It read 80 degrees. The oil pressure was 40 psi and he thought this is a

small car with a long bonnet. Murtyl manoeuvred the car around and after just a few minutes they were out in front of the *Wheat*. "Well lad, we'd better get her out for a run and back and booked in for an MOT. You good to go?" she asked.

"Ready when you are," was his reply as she slipped her into first. They pulled out into the road and she looked left, right and left. The clutch was engaged, they were off. Swiftly they were into second and Nick could hear the wail of the super charger. He wondered what he was in for. One thing was for sure, this thing must produce some serious horses.

Murtyl turned down a lane past a little garage and waved to the mechanic who waved back. She turned her head toward Nick as they approached a bend and winked at him. Double de clutching from fourth to second, she hurried the throttle. Everything changed. Nick grabbed the handrail in front of him as the great beast almost lifted from the ground. The rear tyres screamed in pain as they spun up on the tarmac. The front wheels slid and washed out a little before counter steering became required, then it all went light. Suddenly they were into third gear and were off at a pace Nick did not think was possible for a car from 1956. Every corner was approached differently because it was different. The road was respected and read in a way Nick had never seen. The car seemed to glide effortlessly while drifting, bouncing and protesting all at the same time. This whole routine carried on all the way to Helmsley - 20 miles away. Nothing passed them, neither cars nor bikes and at one point Nick wasn't too sure if the RAF would have had trouble keeping up with them. All the time, she - Murtyl remained relaxed, elegant and in total control. No that was not it, she and the Healy were just working as one unit. Her legs never seemed to stop moving, his eyes were showing him things he had never seen before. The left foot usually

23

depresses and releases the clutch. In her case it did that, but it also did some of the braking with the middle pedal while the right foot remained planted on the throttle. At other times, the right foot and toes did the braking, while the heel of the same foot depressed the accelerator during down changes of the gears. The revs, except whilst idling, at the one junction they had stopped at, never dropped below 4000 rpm.

Nick was in awe of the leg and feet movement. Then he looked at her dainty hands positioned at nine and three o'clock on the steering wheel. The left hand only left the wheel to change gear. The right never left the wheel at all. They supported each other when changing direction. Even on tight bends they stayed locked to the steering wheel. The arms just crossing at the elbows as they rotated the wheel. He began to not actually relax, but realised he was not necessarily heading straight toward a wooden overcoat. He lifted his head and assessed the speeds they were doing. Nothing was overtaken on blind crests or left hand corners. Vehicles were lined up, monitored, and manoeuvred around. Everything seemed to be pre-calculated. He was now beginning to enjoy the fairground ride. He wasn't sure how all the individual parts of her driving fitted together but oh boy, somehow, they did, and the result was the fastest, safest, most scary ride he had ever been on. Tears streamed down his face caused by the buffeting wind hitting his eyes. She had her sunglasses on and was just smiling, occasionally glancing at him, showing those beautiful teeth and that cheeky face that invited him in with, "Is this OK for you or do you want more?" He held his hand up and gesticulated that he was hungry. Her face turned a little sad. In no time they were in Helmsley, parked up and out of the car to go and eat the rolls and soup on a bench. Once perched, they could discuss all the motorcycles parked up, as well as other things.

Before they were too deep in discussion, Nick had one yearning question to ask. He looked at her with puppy dog eyes. She noticed and replied quite abruptly - almost with impatience, "Come on Nick, SPIT it out!" He did so after swallowing the last of the soup in his mouth. "Well it's just I have never experienced or seen anything quite like that before: fast - bloody fast, but safe! I know plenty of quick boys but there are always risks being taken. You took, as far as I could tell, NO risks, everything was calculated and smooth. So the question that I want to know is have you actually taken a driving test - as they don't teach that stuff as far as I know!"

Murtyl sighed. "Yeeeehhhhssss, I do have a license, but I never took a test." He looked confused. She carried on, "When I was young there was no test to speak of, the rules of the road were developing as more motor vehicles appeared. So, when they brought in a driving test, those who had been driving just got a license as they had already been driving. Next question?"

His reply started with, "Oh!" then he paused. "Why do you drive like that and who taught you?"

Murtyl replied, "I don't have to, but I prefer the fun way to the boring way. Robert and Willy taught me early on and after the war my employer liked to keep me up to date with the latest techniques as you just never know when a skill may just come in handy!"

Nick now asked without thinking. "Your employer seemed to like you to be able to respond and move quickly when required, and you obviously can. Why?"

She held a finger up and wagged it at him. "Not ready yet, nice try. You will get everything - that decision has been made, but not until I'm ready. Don't ask again. OK?" Her face was serious.

Nick shuddered within as he knew things were going to come. He nodded and was unsure as to whether he

25

should apologise or not, but inside he was delighted. Sitting on the bench in the village square they looked at the motor bikes and they discussed the pros and cons of two and four stoke engines. One two-stroke passed by and the very slight breeze wafted over the scent of Castrol R. Nick's eyes lit up as his nostrils caressed the whiff of sweetly burnt Castor oil with whatever Castrol had done to it. Murtyl leant back and drew in a great lung full of the odour, then leant forward and breathed out. "One day Nick, one day someone will get that scent into a bottle - every petrol head loves it. It makes my knees turn to jelly every time. I hope someday it happens, there are just so many who have never experienced a bouquet with such a wonderful ability to create the excitement of hot engines and danger. God, I love it!"

Nick smiled, shrugged his shoulders, and commented, "Really, you think that's a winner?"

"Oh yes Nick, in a way you would never believe, it has to be up there with Chanel No 5 and she was a girl who played both sides!"

"I'm sorry I don't understand what you mean?"

"Read your history books Nick, the truth will out in the end. It may not be for a while, but it will come out. No matter how much they try to hide it!" she replied.

"So you really think a girl could fall for that smell then? he asked.

"Oh Yeeeeehhhhs, I did, its beautiful on the right man!" she exclaimed.

"You did?"

"Yeeehhs Nick, I did. The only man I ever loved; a French pilot based at Elvington near York, not too far from here. He was flying Halifax's out over Europe on sadly one too many sorties during WW11. Sadly, I never met another man who could live up to him. Life got to a point where I just focused on being the 'Best of the Best' and then tried to improve - a little like you try to!" She smirked at his face as he suddenly became

26

rather flushed. Nick's mind thought it would be a good time possibly ask some questions. "At what though Murtyl?"

She answered his question but in a fashion he was not expecting. "I worked for the establishment (or government) directly and indirectly on a covert basis from 1943 until recently. Since then, I have put some facts on paper to go with the notes I wrote post operation. These will come to you and you only, as I believe I can trust you to do the right thing with them. You will receive these diaries when the time is correct. You will have to research and verify the details and then write them up. They can only be published if appropriate and people are interested - once the official secrets act allows you to do so. You will be guided in this by a trusted friend. I had to sign that dreaded act so many years ago. I am fluent in French, Swiss German and speak a little smattering of Arabic. It would be wrong for me to tell my story, however if you think my past is worthy of publishing, then I am trusting you to do so. Once you have a diary you will have to research, verify, and fill in the blank areas which at the time were of no concern to me. You will fill in the details to allow readers to understand the greater picture. I have given times, dates, and some names, as well as my personal parts and actions. I assume you are beginning to understand the extent of the task I am entrusting to you?" He nodded in awe of the lady in front of him.

"In the meantime, I expect to have some fun with you - like today. I will help you with your racing and we can do a little travelling! Right lad are you up to driving us home?"

Nick almost jumped forward to answer and would have if he could have got any further forward on his seat.

"Yes, I would love to. Mind you, I can't drive the way you did - I need to keep my license, without it I have no job. So is it OK with you if we kind of go at a sporty / pottering pace!"

He rose and they both headed towards her car. He sat in the driver's seat, inserted, and then turned the key, moved his left hand towards the starter button and pushed it. He released it when the straight six burst into life. He turned his head towards Murtyl as he smiled, "You can trust me with your life you." - know

"I believe I already am!" and she smiled in her glorious way Nick had begun to realise meant mischief as she laughed. As he sedately drove them back to her home, Nick listened intently. "My life is much simpler now compared to my past. When I was young my mother sadly died so my father moved us to Hutton Rudby to stay with his mum as he thought it would give me a more rounded and better up bringing. As they trundled along, she carried on with stories from her childhood, telling him of some of the adventures she had got up to. In what seemed to be no time at all they were back in H.R. and they pulled the car into the garage Murtyl watched him shut the engine down whilst apologising for boring him with her youth.

Nick replied to her," You never bore me Murtyl, you have just done so much and there has to be a history to it all!"

"Ah you're thinking of the good old days. Well I don't remember them as others do." she had replied and then carried on with. "I suppose I became a kind of Civil Servant."

Nick looked at her in surprise as his mind thought of bowler hats and pin stripe suits. "Don't look puzzled Nick, it will become clear but for now, get yourself next door for a beer or two. Remember no talking - I'm off to bed as I need my beauty sleep." He nodded and sidled off to the pub with the broadest grin on his face, while she retired to bed. His mind raced - I still have no idea who she is, what she's done, where, when or why. But bloody hell she must have done something pretty exciting. He couldn't wait for tomorrow.

Chapter 4.
Still in the Dark.

After the few days holiday, Nick returned to work on the Monday morning. He had walked into the open plan office bright and early - for a change and was happy with the few days he had enjoyed spent with his friend Murtyl. As he went through the messages left on his desk, Bill his boss appeared and came over for a chat. Sitting on the corner of Nick's desk, he enquired as to how things were going. Had he enjoyed his few days off and where were they at regarding the story? Bill asked in a roundabout way while adjusting his tie, "Well Nick you have now been visiting Murtyl for several weeks and I presume you have spent the last few days with her. So tell me what you know and when I am going to get to see at least the start of your scoop?" Nick carried on looking at Bill in his clean pressed shirt that somehow was able to make look grubby even though it was fresh on that morning.
"Ah Sir, I wondered when you'd be asking that. Well just now..." He paused, his eyes tried to focus on Bill's face, but struggled due to guilt. "To be honest, I know nothing. I mean I do, she is a great sport, bloody clever and had something to do with the civil service. I have had some extraordinary experiences, but in truth, I know nothing." He began to sweat. "I know as you know there is something big going on, but she is just not ready to talk about whatever it is or was. However I do know that the 'Official Secrets Act' is involved." He stated.
Bill's reply was abrupt, and Nick thought he must be under some pressure from somewhere. "I'm shocked Nick, we are paying you damned good money to be a reporter and we need your story to sell papers. Obviously, I was wrong about you and your ability to get stuck in and get the job done." He explained in the harsher of manner.

30

Nick stood his ground, which was something he probably would not have done prior to meeting Murtyl. "Sir
I am doing my job and well if you must know. If you're
not happy, then I apologise. I can tell you that whatever
it is that she has to give is going to come to us. I just
don't know what it is or when it will happen!"
Bill stood up and walked away from Nick's desk toward his own office. He muttered but in an audible
fashion. "Don't bother anymore, I'll find someone
else!" and then entered his office slamming his door
behind him.
Nick mumbled to himself. "Ooooh he must be under
more pressure than I thought. Idiot, there really is a big
story here. Oh just for a little patience and trust!"

Straight after work he headed out to Murtyl's home to
advise her of his editor's thoughts and decision. In reality it was to warn her and give himself peace of mind,
hoping that she would stand by her word. This way he
would feel much more secure within himself.

He told Murtyl that Bill was intending to send someone
else from the paper to talk to her regarding her story.
Murtyl just rolled her eyes and smiled that fantastic
smile at him and simply remarked. "That's fine Nick."
He relaxed a little. "It means we are not under pressure
and I have more time to prepare you for the information
you are to receive."
Nick shrugged his shoulders a little, "Sorry I don't understand."
"That's OK Nick, I was young and impatient once just
like you. My partner Albert Noir (Berty) and I have
done a few jobs in our time."
Nick impatiently butted in. "But you never told me you
had a partner!" Almost in a pleading voice.
Murtyl burst out laughing. "You are correct, I had not.
Some of these jobs were above and some were below
the water line so to speak."

Nick, like a schoolboy, stuck up his hand to ask a question.

Murtyl ignored it and carried on. "Sadly, we never had the opportunity to marry but together we were all the same." She carried on for a short while and he just kept listening. Then after a while Murtyl suggested that she tell him about a few years of her life. "I believe the world would not be the place it is today if we had not done what we did at the time." Nick was now sitting on the edge of his seat again. She carried on. "Don't take notes, just listen, there'll be time for that later. Just use your memory and allow your imagination to work. I know how retentive it is. You promise me that when the time is right you will get this information into the public domain." Nick nodded solemnly. "I wouldn't like to think the few months I have known you have been wasted! What Berty my team and I have done during the past forty years really should be public knowledge."

Nick swallowed hard while he thought what the hell she could be talking about. All the time his mouth remained closed. Then he blurted out. "Murtyl, you're a nutter in a car, and what is this about My Team?" He thought to himself, Oh God I had no idea today would be the day. I know I am happy to listen, but no notes makes things difficult.

She began in a soft soothing mellow tone. "Step by step, keep it as simple as one two three. Just don't let me down Nick!" Her eyes looked at him in a piercing way.

He answered. "No Murtyl, I couldn't do that. Since meeting you my focus on the track has become better, I listen more intently and work at things more efficiently than ever before!"

"Yeeehhhss you are learning. Listen twice as much as you talk, be aware of being aware and if you think you know, then you don't so shut the hell up until you do!" she replied.

It was still prior to the summer solstice and there was plenty of good strong day light. She glanced out of the dining room window and smiled. "Well I think a ride out to clear my mind while I get everything in an order, so to speak." Nick nodded and they started putting their kit on straight away. They started their bikes and headed out of the village toward Stokesley, then headed via the back roads over towards Danby in the North Yorkshire moors.
Murtyl stayed in front and took things slowly while she settled into the Triumph and the tyres warmed up. Nick followed, knowing she was giving him plenty of time to get through the junctions and keep up. Her Triumph burbled beautifully. Once away from the built up areas, she started to pick her pace up. Her body language told him she was relaxing into the ride as he dutifully followed on roads that were unknown to him. Again her pace picked up as her tyres started to give better feedback now that they were warm and flexing correctly on the tarmac. He thought he would have an advantage on more up to date rubber and twin disc brakes on his front end. However that was not the case, her twin leading front brake was just as efficient as his stoppers. Odd puffs of blue smoke came from her exhaust when she changed gear and on the over run. He was smelling that Castrol R in his head and beginning to understand her statement in Helmsley a few days earlier.

Now tipping her Triumph into bends even more enthusiastically, he was beginning to wonder if he could bloody well keep up with her. What with gravel here and there, and a few damp patches on the road, things were getting a little hairy as far as he was concerned. Yet she just kept on at that pace effortlessly, it just seemed to suit her style. Going over humps in the road

33

and sharp bridges she either had her front wheel off the
ground or both of the ruddy things. Her bike seemed to
rev a little higher than he had expected from a British
classic. He expected a thump from the long stroke parallel twin cylinder. The noise he actually heard was
more of a deep thrapping sound that was like thunder.
She even got the odd slide on mid corner. Her inside
leg would hover just off the foot peg and then drop an
inch or two toward the ground offering possible security. The throttle would be teased on; the rear wheel
would start to spin up rather than slide. This drove the
motorcycle forward while she naturally counter steered.
It was beautiful to see and was being done so well it
was almost like being at an exhibition. He was now just
clinging onto her shirt tails so to speak and had nearly
fallen off his bike as he was spending so much time
watching her. He really did have so much to learn from
her. Then calmly after going through the village of
Danby, she pulled over by a gate. It was open and she
rode through it. He
followed; she rode to a slight bank and stepped off her
bike leaning against the bank side. She turned her fuel
tap off and started walking. He followed suit.

She stood waited for him, beckoning him over. The
view of the dale was magnificent and the meadow they
were in was just amazing - long grass smattered with
meadow flowers. He could hear curlews calling and
swifts were darting hither and thither after their prey.
She walked on and he followed her toward a line of
trees that he could only assume followed the river Esk
which would be flowing out towards Whitby and the
North Sea.

As they got closer to the tree line, Murtyl stared to kick
her boots off followed by her socks. Now she was bare
foot and Nick started to wonder what she was doing.
Her jacket was then peeled off and dropped on the

34

deck. Her helmet and gloves had been left by her bike, as was Nick's. However, he was not taking his clothes off. Then her blouse was unbuttoned and still nothing was said as it dropped to the meadow floor. He now started to drop back a little as she loosened her belt and when her pants dropped and were left behind her, he began to have thoughts of. "I can't believe this. I know she is worldly, and I do know a few girls who like a bit of fun, but she's in her bloody sixties. I mean I love her loads but not like this." He ceased walking and sat. As he did so she held her left hand out showing her palm as if to say stop. He hadn't really seen the command as his mind was elsewhere in his imagination and he had stopped anyway. She went down, head down and arse up, moving more slowly to the tree line in a stealth like fashion. He calmed and thought maybe she wants to go swimming, but either way his head was gone in a flight of panic.

Once at the tree line he could see her drop a few feet and presumed she was now paddling in the cold water of the river Esk. She obviously knew where she was and what she was doing. He watched from a distance not daring to think of what was going to happen next and realised she had not asked him to take his clothes off, yet.

Bent over double, she seemed to shimmy along up the river against its flow. Every few minutes she would rise a little, bring her arms and hands up and rub them together. Then she just started the same exercise again. Nick remained dumbfounded and sceptical. Neither spoke a word, her due to concentration, and him for fear of entrapment. Surely, she didn't expect him to do IT as it were, with him, in a bloody field.

Her ritual carried on for another six or seven minutes. To him it felt like a lifetime of anxiety. Then all of a sudden, her head turned towards him and the hair followed in a flowing fashion. That broad incredible smile appeared, and he was sure she was winking at him. Then she stood up, smoothly but firmly, her arms followed suit with an object between her hands. The object became a missile which was thrown whole heartedly towards him. He ducked and closed his eyes, wondering what on earth she had found. A single word followed this procedure, loud and clear. "Dinner!"

He looked up and just a few feet away from his head was a great big bloody brown trout of just under two pounds flapping away in front of him. He felt exhausted, stupid and he didn't know where to place his shame after letting so many crazy thoughts run through his mind. Under his breath he said to himself, "You stupid idiot!" and then relaxed as she climbed out of the water.

In her knickers and bra she strode towards him in that Murtyl way. Hips a swaying and relaxed as ever with that great big happy smile. His astonished, shocked smile told her all, and she said gently to him. "You're hot Nick but not that hot. Dinner is caught, and once cooked, I will explain what I was doing." She laughed at the expression on his face - knowing what he must have been thinking. "Come on lad, let's get our gear on, go home and cook this chap for dinner. Butter, parsley and some new potatoes sounds just the ticket!"
Shakily he got to his feet and followed her, carrying the trout as she dressed while they walked back to their bikes.

They rode home in the same fashion they had got to the place she had caught the trout. Nick was having trouble keeping up as his concentration was not up to scratch. Murtyl just hit her pace and was going like the clappers. Two wheel drifting, sliding, and taking off here

36

and there. Half the time road racing style and the other
half riding in the style of a scrambler. Nick eventually
pulled himself together and got on her tail. Using every
ounce of skill and power his bike had, he still only just
stayed with her. As the pace cooled down on entry to
Hutton Rudby speed limits, Nick caught his breath.
Running through his mind as the sweat ran down his
face inside his helmet, was what is she? Clean, tidy, and
beautiful: YES! A complete nutter when on the road,
and it would seem fearless, and yet with a mechanical
sympathy and understanding he had never seen before.
Definitely all female, and he did mean really all female.
Now she's catching bloody fish with her sodding hands.
What the hell is she?'

Now back at the cottage and with the bikes parked up,
Murtyl went inside, upstairs and changed. Nick did so
out in the yard and gutted the trout as instructed. Murtyl
returned with a knee length pleated skirt on that sat on
her hips in that, well to Nick, sexy fashion. Her blouse
was of the 'I live in the country' style and was cotton in
a light cream colour with fine lines that made out small
checks. It was buttoned up from the waist to the top
three buttons and her hair flowed down. He noted no
tights or stockings but pop socks and brown brogue
shoes. He realised how he was looking at her and his
mind thought back to being in the meadow just a few
hours ago. Bloody hell, he thought, I want it, I don't
want it, I know I shouldn't, then think I should. I really
do need to get control of my bloody imagination and
hormones. But that way she moves does make it difficult!'

He lit the little makeshift barbecue - home made from
an old gas bottle cut in half length ways. In the bottom
were a few holes that had been drilled to allow air in
from underneath. There were flaps to control that flow.
Inside there were two grates. The lower one for the

charcoal to sit on and a top one for the food to be cooked on the lie.

The unit lit, and when up to temperature, they started the cooking process. The new potatoes in a small pan with water was placed on the makeshift cooker. Once boiling, they had to wait ten minutes. When the spuds were almost cooked, some peas joined them in the same pan. Now the filleted fish went on the grate - flesh side down toward the searing heat. It sizzled and steamed, dribbling all at the same time. The odour was different: charcoaling burnt meat, tinged with river and cooking meat. Once Murtyl was satisfied - after around three minutes, the trout was turned over. Soon the skin was going crispy. While that was happening, copious amounts of fresh butter and parsley were lathered onto the upper side of the fish. Their plates were heated with the water drained off from the peas and potatoes. Once dried, they are ready to plate up. More butter with salt n pepper made this up to be one of the best meals Nick had ever eaten. "What a bloody day!' ran through his mind.

He now understood as she had explained a while ago, that he had been born with two ears and one gob. If he wasn't sure of his facts, then he didn't know. So shutting up and listening was the way forward. He also knew now in his heart, that whatever she was going to tell him was going to have a profound effect on the rest of his life. Then she started to talk.

"I grew up in this village a few generations ago. Most of the people I knew left during the war years and sadly only a few of them returned. My best friend was Cerian, she was beautiful, crazy and such good fun to be around." Murtyl smiled and carried on. "She was always smiling, laughing, and joking about everything. We liked to play tricks on each other too, in between

doing all sorts of mischief. She was the only girl I played with; all our real friend were boys. Cerian was so quick witted, sarcastic, and funny without knowing it. She had us all laughing at school, in lessons and on the green out there. We'd be five or six years old then. Life was just fun, we fought our fights, stole apples and if there was trouble to be had, we would be first to find it. Cerian had long blonde hair, dark blue eyes, and a stunning smile to which I know she broke a few hearts as life progressed. She had the quickest mind and a merciless sense of humour I have ever come across. She would just have me in stitches with her unrelenting cheek!" Murtyl carried on talking with Nick just taking it all in. "I have some images on print of us all during those times. Would you like to see some?"
"Oh yes Murtyl, I'd love to."

During this conversation, they had cleaned up and moved into the lounge. Sitting on the maroon sofa and relaxing, they chatted. Murtyl's left hand raised and then went down to the left of the sofa and brought up an old, worn, battered folder. He wondered what he was going to be shown and whether her life was then as crazy as she seemed to be now.

Chapter 5
The early years and some tom boy fun.

On the great round oak coffee table Murtyl began to
spread out the photographs while Nick was sent away
to make a pot of tea. As he returned it would seem they
had been quickly set out in date order. Nick knew to
expect nothing less from this great lady. However he
did notice her grinning at a few of the images in front
of her.
"I was such a tom boy when I was younger you know."
Murtyl smiled. Nick replied in his best shocked tone,
"Really?"
"I was more interested in building things and racing
carts going down that hill out there, than doing femin-
ine things." She continued.

The first load of photographs were put away then the
next batch came out and were arranged in a similar
fashion. "Have a look at these now."
One by one he studied them. Of course none were in
colour, and they were yellowed and a bit dusty; however he could make out most of the people and he could
see they were having a great time. "It looks to me as
you must have had the best of childhoods with that
group of misfits." Nick suggested.
"Yeeehhhs, I think I did!" she answered. And then
paused.
Nick pointed to a few specific pictures and asked, "Did
you build that?" she peered at the few pictures being
pointed at and answered, "Yeeehhhs, that was the day
Cerian and I decided to take the big boys on and race
them from the top of the green all the way down over
the river, which was the finish line. I beat them all that
day - my first ever win!" She laughed at the thought of
it.

"You give the impression …." he paused.

"Go on lad, spit it out!' She smirked as she wondered what his question was going involve.

"Well you seem to give me the impression that other than being very, very strong minded, you never give in or let life get you down." He stated as he smiled at her. "Correct, life is too short, and you have to live it in the now, as you never know what is around the corner, or what life is going to deal you next. Anyhow, you are staying again tonight? I'd be glad of the company." she asked. He nodded and they carried on chatting all evening over a few more brews.

"I know you must be wondering Nick why I seem to be able to do some of the things you have watched me do in the past few days." Murtyl commented.
"Yeeehhhs…" He answered in that new way of using that word to him. "I have been flummoxed with the way you seem to perform at times."

"I can see that Nick. My father was a busy man travelling Europe, he had survived WW1 in the military and was very well to do, so to speak. After WW1 he became a negotiator for the British, selling arms mainly in Europe but occasionally in Africa too. During the longer school holidays, he would take me with him if it were possible. From the age of twelve or so he taught me to maintain and fire most small arms; to tickle fish; snare game; how to defend myself and survive. He seemed to know WW11 was going to happen, and I believe he was doing his best to prepare and protect me, or at least give me a fighting chance if the UK was ever invaded. I could, in my day, shoot the ace out of a playing card at 250 yards with no eye assistance - not too shabby!" She then continued, "So my father and I lived with my gran in this house. When he was away and when he was home, Cerian and I got up to a lot of no good. We competed with the boys at everything. We out poached, out trapped and snared game and were just as good at them at everything.

Once we did get caught by a gamekeeper. He took us to my gran who gave me a good wallop on the backside. Not so much for poaching but for the fact we had been caught. That's when it dawned on me, if you're not going to get caught, you need to be the 'Best of the Best' and keep improving. The gamekeeper's name was Kevin Mooney - I really liked him. As time went on Kev took us under his wing. Now he was a good one, he was good with horses too. On the day he caught us, we - or at least I, thought we had the measure of him. We never thought he could jump his horse over several five bar gates and a few high Hawthorn hedges to come round and catch us from where we were in relation to him. However he did and he got in front of us. As he befriended us, he taught us how not to get caught. It turned out he supplemented his income, not by selling meat etc to butchers and others, but he did so by riding as a jockey in a lot of point to point races. He got us to spend bets for him on himself, in exchange for teaching us all the best poachers' tricks: how not to be caught by having an eye for detail; animals have great sniffers and can smell you've been there. Then there was the details: leave no trace of your actions; everything you touch must be mentally noted and replaced in exactly the same way, otherwise whatever it you've been unto will find a way to go wrong and come back and bite your bottom. Anything we caught or he had extra, we got to take home. My Gran and Cerian's mum were always grateful. I am sure they knew Kev was keeping an eye on it all and we never got greedy. He was really softly spoken - a small man who was big in stature. He had tanned skin and his hair had a side parting, you could never fine a gentler kinder friend. He was really good with those horses too. He was sharp as they come with steely blue eyes. He never missed a damned thing such was his eye for detail. He went away for a few nights

42

with his wife once, we borrowed a few snags and traps
and went to work, as it were. We made sure we placed
them back in exactly the correct position - cleaned and
just right! Not a thing was out of order. The bugger still
had us for it though. That is where I really learnt the
first rule: detail, detail, detail. The big picture will
come together if the detail is right." Murtyl took a
breath and laughed.

Chapter 6.
Travelling and meeting Berty.

"Anyway as got a little older I was doing OK at school;
however I did have a little trouble with languages. This
was when my father decided to start taking me away a
regular basis. He seemed to know everybody of import-
ance wherever we were. If there was a big social event,
we were at it with the important people - if you know
what I mean." Nick nodded in silence. "I loved going to
the Grand Prix and watching the cars. This was where I
was introduced to the great Willy Grover Williams (and
his wife Yvonne) and Robert Benoist. These two were
the great Bugatti works drivers based in Paris. Then
there was Jean Pierre Wimille - their protégé, and his
soon to be wife Cric. I was often left with them for a
few days when dad had special meetings to go to. Now
they were, when I think about it, great days: 1933 to
1938. I was in and out of Bugatti dealerships all over
France with the great drivers. At race meeting I was
treated like a princess. Robert and Willy taught me to
drive in my first ever car which they had bought for me
- a 1932 Austin Seven, I competed in some races and
hill climbs under their instruction with some success.
You haven't seen her yet Nick: gun metal grey over old
English white and still ready to race. I keep her just up
the road in Gary's garage I'll take you up to see her
soon and take you out for a spin.

Robert Benoist was a pilot during WW1, in fact he was
noted as a daredevil (ace) fighter pilot. Once I knew
this I pushed and pushed him for a flight with him.
Eventually he did take me up. He tried and tried to
break me, not a glimmer of hope could he achieve, with
all his manoeuvres, to cause me to throw up or hold my
hands in the air to suggest I had had enough. What a
ride that was: brilliant." Nick could see the excitement
and joy whirling out of her eyes toward him. She car-

44

ried on. "After much pestering he gave in and taught me to fly, it was great fun and stood me in good stead for the ATA only a few years later. I think I had my wings before I even drove a car on the left hand side of the road."

Nick interrupted her. "I think I can see where most of these pictures have come from, but why have I never heard of these three guys you've mentioned before?"

Murtyl picked and answered. "Well, there is no denying Willy and Robert were the best of the best in their day. Sadly, they never got to show how good they were in the fifties against the like of Fangio. The Nazi SS made sure of that, following Hitler's special instructions of 'Night Fog' during the latter days of WW11.

It seemed to Nick that the night was one of 'those' nights. She just seemed to want to talk so he sat there and listened. "When I was twelve or thirteen and dad went to Spain or on to Africa, he usually left me with the 'Noirs' in Marseille in Southern France. Mr Noir was a diplomatic lever as chief of the Police in that region. I got on well with his son Albert.

The other children used to torture the two of us for being posh and well off compared to them. It didn't take long for us to find out we worked well together after being in many tight squeezes. We seemed to know what each other was thinking when we were in one of those tight spots. Our actions just seem to work in a complimentary fashion with each other. He was good with his hands and I was improving all the time. He even taught me to use a bowline and a sling once he knew I could poach and trap. I was able to show him a few of the tricks Cerian and I had picked up from Kevin, these things seemed to cement our friendship for the future.

"Sadly, it all came to an end when tensions in Europe became too great. Chamberlain said

'There would be peace in our time' as we all knew there had been unbelievable nastiness in Germany as Hitler and his Nazi's took over and prepared their war machine. The German teams came out with their incredible Nazi financing of original Mercedes and the AUs.

Willy completed bravely against them in his Bugatti at the 1936 Monaco Grand Prix. For the last few laps he was stuck in top gear and yet still brought his machine home ahead of them to win.

Once the invasion of Poland started in 1939, nearly all the Brits flooded back to the UK. Sadly, I soon lost contact with the 'Noirs, Benoits and Grover Williams.' I had to concentrate on doing what I could at home. I started as a land girl to do my part for the war effort and worked my heart out. The farmer I worked for soon realised I was pretty good at getting engines running and I could drive. He reported this and the next thing I knew I was driving ambulances. It soon came out in discussion at an aerodrome, when some aircraft were near an incident and I moved then out of danger, that I had done bit of flying in my time. Within just a few days I was moved to yet another uniform and started to fly for the ATA (Air Transport Auxiliary) delivering aircraft from repair and new builds, to their station of operation. We never got to carry live ammunition which I thought was a bit rubbish. Once or twice, on route to Biggin Hill and Manston with fighters, I was attacked by German fighters. I managed to elude the fighters using the crazy skill Robert had been so kind to tutor me in.

It was damned hard work getting into different aircraft. Anything from single engine to four engine beasts. Working from a one-page-per-aircraft note pad that gave: 'start up, take off, cruise and landing procedures' only. We were expected to pick up and deliver whatever

46

the aeroplane was, to its destination, navigating yourself on the way. Once you landed safely at the destination and the aircraft was signed for, you were turfed out quick smart. Once off the aerodrome, we were expected to find our own way to our next pick up and take that to its designated squadron. I loved it; the pressures were intense. Of course there were days with the old tail dragging aircraft, where windspeed across the runway where you were or at your destination, was outside the aircraft limits for take-off and landing. Then there the days when visibility was too poor. On those days we were left to entertain ourselves. On these occasions I tended to go for walks and catch, poach or in truth, steel anything I could. We were just always so damned hungry on those rations. It seemed to come about most places I appeared, there would often be a little bit of a buzz if the weather were a bit off. I later realised that everybody else was hungry too and when I appeared, they used have some sort of system to bet what kind of food I would appear with after my walk out. Cheeky buggers!

One particular day I was delivering a Halifax four engine bomber to Elvington operational airfield just outsider of York; I came down and landed, thinking bloody marvellous, I might just get a couple of days at home as its only 25miles from here. I could get the train from York to Thirsk then get off at Yarm and walk from there. As it happened, I taxied the aircraft in at around 1800 hours, shut her engines down, all mags off - fuel and electrical circuits and I alighted the aircraft. While I was walking across the apron towards the control tower to get my logbook signed, I nearly fell to my knees as my stomach churned and turned over. I didn't understand at first, as I turned and grimaced, I saw Albert Noirs heading out to an aircraft that was flying out on a mission that evening. I just prayed that he'd be coming back safe as I now realised, I loved him."

Murtyl paused for a few moments and took a sip of her now cold tea and sort to catch her breath, "I went to see the squadron commander very briefly, knocked on his door, I knew this wasn't the done thing, but I needed to confirm what I already knew. He answered my knock with the word 'Enter' in the most unbelievably, highly educated kind of stuffy tone. The Wing Commander sat there, leant back in his chair with his tie done up tight and his classic Royal Air Force style moustache, black hair crew cut with neatly trimmed short sideburns, sporting a bit of a tan as it was towards the spring. As he looked me up and down, I noticed he was a bloody big fella, guessing he must be at least 6ft 2" and a little portly, it seemed he had decided himself that he was a cut above me, but that didn't matter. I had to know, was that Albert? I said to him, 'Excuse me Sir, I've just dropped off your aircraft and am leaving to go home, I know this is a French squadron and there is information you cannot give me, but I think I saw an old family friend, Albert Noir, could it really be him?' The commander replied in his deep baritone voice, 'I cannot confirm nor deny that we have a wonderful pilot by that name,' and he winked his left eye at me. My heart fluttered; I knew the bastard was here. He stoked and lit his pipe, pulling the flame deep into the tobacco, puffing plumes of fragrant blue grey smoke - it stank! Murtyl winked at Nick and continued the story. The commander was tapping a rhythm with his left index finger on his desk; 'If someone was to leave their contact details on a piece of paper, on my desk, and that person you asked about actually existed, it may just find its way to him.' He smiled knowingly at me, while pushing a pencil and piece of paper across his desk. I jotted my name and address on the paper and slid it back in the Wing Commander's direction. I spotted the name plate on his desk and then told Wing Commander Jack Butler that I was much obliged. He nodded in ac-

48

knowledgement and gestured with his hand for me to leave and mumbled 'I've not seen you here' as I exited the office. Jack later became a lifelong friend and was often a go between, for later operations with various sovereign states. His personal intermediary and liaison skills even saved my bacon a few times. He was also damned good fun to be with when he was off duty!"

She paused again for a few seconds. "So Nick, at that point I had a couple of days off and spent them at home with my Gran, fettling my Father's motorbike, knowing this would be the best form of transport. I knew Berty was definitely in the U.K., but I didn't want to get my hopes up in case he never made contact. Over the next couple of days, two men in business suits and bowler hats, both holding brolly's, knocked on the door as they did every two months and asked if there was a letter for them. There would usually be a letter from my father every two, three or four weeks to my Gran and I, plus a third letter that would come alternately addressed to my Gran and myself except this had a number '5' on it – this was for the men that came. The first one we ever received was a little note to us from my Father, to say that any envelope which came from him, with the number five in the address was not for us. These letters would be picked up by London businessmen. I believed they were actually intelligence people, because one month a letter would be from Lisbon and a while later, they would come from Switzerland. Six or nine months after that they would appear from Australia and I still don't really know what he did - not fully anyway. The gentlemen before leaving, would always say, 'Thank you ma'am. We would just like to let you know that your person of interest is safe'. This went on throughout the war until one day they came and did not say he was safe but had to regretfully inform us that the person we were interested in (being my father), would not be returning. Sadly, I never found out what he did, how he

49

did it, when he did it, or where he did what he did. Later, when I left the ATA and joined the Special Operations Executive (S.O.E.) I found out that he had been a highly respected man."

Chapter 7. The Times, MI5 and S.O.E.- Murtyl's working life.

"Sorry this is taking a long time; this is not even half of it. Do you want me to continue?" Nick answered straight away, "I would love nothing better Murtyl, I'm hooked!" She took another sip of her cold tea and she continued where she left off, "The day after that, I received a telegram which made my heart sing, because in those days, telegrams tended to be bad news. But it read 'Gifted three day pass STOP HR tonight 1900. STOP Berty.' I slapped my thigh with my hand, while having the biggest grin on my face and replied back 'Please reply, "Merci" STOP. I literally jumped for joy, ran back to the house, grabbed my Gran, and told her she would finally meet Berty - the boy I fell in love with. I squeezed her so tight that day, I stood back, and she saw the light in my eye; and then I was shaking – she could read me like a book my Gran. She glanced me up and down, winked at me and said, 'If it's right lass, it's right.' Then she told me to turn tail, get changed, get on to Kevin's beat and get something special for dinner. I came back three hours later with two brace of
partridge: I was that excited I made Kevin a few brews and told him all about Berty!" Murtyl laughed, "I can remember it like it was yesterday! Strange that the brain never shuts off isn't it?"

Murtyl gave him no time to answer, Nick quickly nodded before she continued, "At 13 years old when I first met Berty, my Father (as he had done before), had left me with a family I did not know. But rather than it being with Willy Williams, Robert Benoist or Jean-Pierre Wimille, this time, it was with Berty's parents. Berty's father was the police commissioner for Marseilles and he over saw over the customs. Marseilles was a hard city as it had many, many nationalities there being a seaport, strangers were continuously in and out. At first when I stayed there it felt almost like a military camp; but once it was explained what his father did for a living, I began to understand the difficulties they had in life from various factions and people who were either smugglers, cut throats, vagabonds, thieves or spies. Berty and I would pretend that we were special agents after listening to plays on the wireless. We would re-enact the various plays that were broadcasted, this involved hand to hand combat which we became quite skilful at; through the use of books and practice, and occasionally his father would invite the head of Combat Training instruction for the police to afternoon tea. We would get him, whenever we could, to train and develop our knowledge and skills. We did this for the month that I got to spend with them every year; we seemed to develop an almost instinctive or telepathic ability to know what the other was thinking. Occasionally, when we left the grounds of his father's property, we would be taunted by the local kids. They would attempt to guide us into an area where they could provoke a fight. The intention was really to nick some of our clothes and any money we may have had. The two times we were cornered, we fought our way out and left a right bloody mess behind us. Berty's father did take us to one side and explained to us how privileged we were in our upbringing, skill sets, speed of thought and reasoning. Later in life, if what he feared was to come about, we would be very glad of the tools we were learning. He slapped us both round the back of the head and stated, 'but don't bloody well use them on my patch.' He was so stern with us that day." Murtyl barely came up for air, she was definitely on a mission to reveal most of her life to Nick. "Bless my Gran, she set off cooking the birds after I'd plucked and dressed them. I climbed the stairs, washed, and put my Sunday best on. I painted the Nylons lines down the back of my legs, as was done in those days, because nobody could get hold of the real things except the Americans. Then I decided it was 'not me' to be dressed up like a dog's dinner, so I washed my legs and got changed again - putting my slacks on and a blouse and then did the best I could with my hair. After that I set off for the bugger. It was around 1840hrs and was too late to go and pick him up, even if I had the fuel to put into father's bike. So I dropped into the Wheat sheaf next door and told the Landlady Jo who was coming. She had listened to my adventures with Berty since I was 13 or 14 years old and was quite excited to meet him. Jo had been left the pub when her partner had been hit in Flanders during the First World War. She never talked about it. The village had lost quite a few men in those sad days. She gave me a drink of lemonade and listened to my excited drivel, which I know helped me relax. I think this was the first time I was ever nervous. Jo was really good to my Gran and I, if there was any food left over from the pub when I was away, she made sure my Gran got the lion's share - in exchange for a bit of cleaning, spud peeling and general help around the place. For me, it meant I knew someone was looking out for my wonderful Gran while I was away working. After speaking to Jo for some time, it was 1915hrs, so I set off up the village, and dropped into the Kings Head. As I said before I never took to drink but old Wrightson the landlord knew me well, as he liked his bikes too. If there were a chance, we would ride out together over the moors and occasionally race each other on top of Carlton Bank where we had a pretty rough but fun scrambles track laid out. A bit of elbowing and kicking used to go on, the trophies were pretty even over the years. He was trying to talk bikes and tell me about the recent raid on Tees port and the Steel Foundry's, but I just blurted on about Berty. Then I told him I had to leave sharpish and I was off but was not too sure how to meet or where to meet him. I ended up by the little memorial at the top of the village for the heroic men lost in WW1 and sat just waiting to hear his footsteps. After ten minutes or so, my tummy started to churn, and I felt a bit sick. I heard a faint whistle coming from along the road toward Craythorne, at first I didn't recognise the tune - then it dawned on me, it was the old French song his Father used to play most evenings when I stayed in Marseilles."

Nick interjected "And then what Murtyl?" Murtyl carried on speaking.

"Instinctively I got up and started to run towards the whistle, he must have seen me before I saw him, because he was running towards me too. As we got really close, we both stopped and just looked each other up and down. He had grown into a really good-looking man and had definitely lost his boyishness. He let out the loudest wolf whistle I had ever heard. He then put both arms out and I ran into them, kicked both legs up into the air and wrapping them around his waist. He spun around, I cried with joy and promptly began to look a real mess. He just kept saying, 'I prayed you'd find me Mon-Cheri. Always together now, always! No matter the situation we work as one to love and protect each other.' We kissed for the first time ever, then strode through the village hand in hand, to my home and Gran for dinner." Murtyl yawned, "I'm getting tired you know lad, but there is so much I need to tell you about Berty and I. Nick's eyes were wide open. "I am all ears Murtyl." He smiled softly at her and waited for her to continue, "Berty and I, we were one of a kind. We knew after the first kiss, that we were meant to be, we ended up spending the next 72 hours together. I showed him around the village and introduced him to all the people there – they loved his sense of humour and his loveable character. We went hunting together and caught all sorts of things in many different kinds of traps. I told him I had a good teacher. I introduced him

54

to the game keeper, Kevin Mooney. The night I introduced Kev and Berty to each other, I found out an answer I had being wanting to know for so long, Kev told
me the secret to his riding ability. I would never have
guessed in a million years, he used to ride King George
V Steeple Chase horses! He was one of the best jockeys
back in his day. He was asked by King George's trainer
to ride in the Gold Cup. I couldn't believe my ears
when he told us, we had to explain it to Berty – I don't
think he understood what the Gold Cup was, but Kev
waffled about it so long I think Berty felt he had ran it
himself by the time the conversation had ended!"
Murtyl yawned again, her eyes getting heavier. "Just a
little while longer then I am going to have to get some
beauty sleep!" Nick folded his arms up and rested his
head on them, gazing into her eyes and watching her
nose move a little as she spoke. He felt like he was with
her in these adventures, the way she described them to
him, "You are an amazing lady Murtyl, you are truly
inspiring - I don't know how you do it." Murtyl looked
over at him and winked.
"Not all me, I couldn't have done most of the things I
have done without Berty. He has been with me through
thick and thin, that man. My life would be nothing
without him in it." Nick at this point wondered if Berty
was still alive, but then thought, well he can't be alive
otherwise he would be in the house and he would have
met him already. He didn't interrupt Murtyl with his
thought and let her continue, "Anyway, when Kevin
told me about how he got into the horse riding career
and how he'd worked alongside King George V with
his horses, under the Royal trainer: Mr Fulke Walwyn.
He gave Berty and me a right old earful about the Gold
Cup. t must have been a jolly good experience for him,
sure sounded like it, the way he was talking. I got Kevin to talk me through the race just a few years ago and
recorded it on to a Dictaphone. "You want to listen to it
then? It goes on for a few minutes if you're interested?"

55

Murtyl asked, "Of course Murtyl, I would love to."
Nick eyes lit up once again and his ears pricked up
ready for it to start. Murtyl pressed the buttons on the
Dictaphone and Kevin Mooney's voice started to come
out of the speaker. It came through clearly and precisely with its Lambourn roll and went like this:

"I was approached in the Spring to ride one of King
George V's horses in the Whitbread Gold Cup at Sandown. My horse was Special Cargo who was trained by
the Royal Trainer, Mr Fulke Walwyn. I was very excited about the chance to ride the horse for the King
George V as it was at one of his favourite courses and
Special Cargo had won there 4 times before, so he
knew his way around. His good quick jumping suited
the track as well as the fences, that came together very
quick down the back straight. However, there would be
another obstacle to contend with, the favourite in the
race 'Diamond Edge' was from the same stable, a horse
that had won the Whitbread Gold Cup twice before,
and so was going for his third. Both horses, especially
Diamond Edge suffered badly with leg injuries, this had
kept them off the track for the last two seasons. They
were trained to the minute, in the weeks leading up to
the race. The ground had been drying out which was a
problem for Special Cargo as he was preferred soft
ground. However, Diamond Edge even with his fragile
legs loved good fast ground. There was a chance Special Cargo may not run if no rain came. As it was, it did
not! As the race got closer King George V and Mr
Walwyn decided that Special Cargo should take his
chance.

On the day of the race, I rode out first lot at Mr Walwyn's just to calm my nerves; this was the biggest
chance of my riding career. After riding out, I cycled
home, on the short journey I kept riding the race in my
head over and over again, hoping that the horse would

handle the fast ground, he might not like it, but at least it would be on the track he loved.

Soon it was time to set off to Sandown Park. Travelling with me in the motor car provided was my wife Sharon and my father; they tried to fill me with confidence. We arrived at Sandown about an hour before the first race, it was a very hot day, and the crowd was massive. In the weighing room there was a real buzz, my nerves were getting to me. The valet who looked after the jockeys had all our tack and silks hanging ready. Mine were the famous blue, buff colours and black cap with gold tassels. It was time to get ready, just to put the royal colours on was a real privilege and an honour for a local lad, born and bred in Lambourn. With the royal colours on it was time to weigh out and get some advice from Mr Fulke Walwyn.

Back in the weighing room there was excitement, nerves and talk about how the race might be run between the other Jockeys. The bell then rang, and it was time to go out to the paddock and meet the royal party with Special Cargo. On arriving in the paddock, King George V and Mr Walwyn put me at ease straight away by saying "Just enjoy the occasion, have a safe ride but if Special Cargo is not enjoying the fast ground, just look after him." Both horses looked magnificent in the sun split sky and the huge crowd really got behind the King George V and wanted him to do well. Nerves were taking over when the bell rang for jockeys to mount, once on his back all was calm. In the parade before the race, Special Cargo was bouncing and felt really well under me.

Soon we were at the start, 3 miles 5 furlongs, 2 ½ circuits of Sandown and 26 fences to jump on fast ground. We were called to make a line and soon we were racing to the first. My plan was to be handy, up in the first 3 or 4 all the way, equally Diamond Edge was up there as well, the first circuit went to plan. However, on passing

57

the stands for the final circuit the pace began to quicken and Special Cargo was beginning to lose his place on the fast ground, but still his jumping was quick so I felt if we could keep in touch, we still had a chance of running well, if not winning. Halfway down the back, Diamond Edge had taken up the running and was jumping well on the hard ground. Turning out of the back straight Special Cargo was only 7th but was slowly getting back to the leaders. Jumping the pond fence (the third last) we saved ground by keeping to the rail, coming off the turn we were in 5th place and starting to close. If we could jump the 2nd last well, we would be close enough to get placed. However we got too close, but we managed not to lose the vital momentum you need for the uphill finish. At the last there were three in a line, Diamond Edge in the middle. We were back in fourth but a good jump at the last, and quickly into his stride we would be right there with a chance of winning. With all four horses and jockeys riding for the line, it went to a three way photograph, the excitement from the crowd was overwhelming. They had just witnessed probably one of the best finishes of the Whitbread Gold Cup ever.

On the long way back to the paddock there had been no announcement of the result, when we had nearly reached the unsaddling enclosure, it came. The winner's name boomed out the loudspeakers, it was 'Special Cargo' who had won by a short head in front of Diamond Edge. Unsaddling Special Cargo and waiting for King George V to arrive, tears of joy were welling in my eyes; the horse with the delicate legs had overcome the fast ground and had carried him faster than the other eleven horses. Then King George VI arrived in the winning enclosure with Mr Walwyn, the excitement was overwhelming for everyone. After weighing in, Sharon, my father and I were invited to the Royal Box to talk through the race with King George VI at length.

Three weeks after the race the yard was still buzzing with excitement when we received a phone call from Windsor Castle. King George VI was to have a private dinner party in London at the home of Colonel Whitbread and his wife for 10 people. In the first conversation it was for myself, my wife, Bill Smith (Diamond Edge's Jockey) and his wife to attend, but unfortunately 1 week before the dinner party was taking place the phone rang again asking if our wives could drop out as the King wanted to invite his daughters.

The Whitbread was the last ride for Bill Smith as he retired on that day and I then became No 1 Jockey for Mr Fulke Walwyn and King George VI on the strength of the Special Cargo ride.'

"What did you think to that then?" Murtyl waited for Nick's response.

"Brilliant, just brilliant! By golly it must have been a real honour to ride one of the King's horses and win the Gold Cup! Bet he had a whale of a time that day, one he will never forget I am sure!" Nick exclaimed.

"Well, he did teach me a thing or two about how to ride a horse, he also taught me how to catch a wild one and break it in. He made them follow him all over, without any halter on or anything. I used to call him the horse whisperer, it was a running joke we had. It was magical, still to this day I don't know how he did it. He was very fair but firm with them and they seemed to have a mutual agreement with him, they treated him as if he were at the top of their pecking order." Murtyl seemed lost in her thoughts – just for a second, before she continued. "Before we knew it Berty was called to Elvington in York on a mission..." Murtyl paused and took a deep breath; Nick didn't know what to expect next, "Was it bad news Murtyl? The mission? Did he succeed?" Murtyl had a tear in her eye at this point but she managed to swallow the lump in her throat and carried on telling Nick what happened, after all he needed to know so he could write about it all when she had gone. "Well, he went over to the German and French borders, he was attacking there and was shot down. The lads think they spotted parachutes come from his Halifax, but no one could verify he was alive, a prisoner of war, or if he were on the run. Berty had no family left, just me. His mother and father were imprisoned by the French Police under the Vichy government who were instructed by the Gestapo, and later murdered by them – he was devastated when he got the news, I think a part of him wanted revenge. I don't know how he managed to stay calm, I think that is why we both worked well together, I was a bit of a hot head in my time and he seemed to be the only one that could hold it all together for me. There will never be another like him, one in a million. When I got word that he was missing, I needed a way to get to France to try and find him. We seemed to feel each other's pain, fear and trouble so I knew in my heart, Berty was in trouble but I also knew he couldn't be dead."

Murtyl looked up at Nick, she had a tear in her eye as he spoke to her, "You don't have to tell me today you know Murtyl, if you don't feel like speaking about it anymore, shall we talk about something else?"
"It was a sad time. I still had contacts through my father, Jack Butler and from some of the interviews I had had before. So I spoke to them and ended up joining up. Because I could speak a few languages, I was offered a desk job at Bletchley Park. I refused it and told a few of my intentions - would they know of any active service that could use me? You see, I was willing to train to whatever level at whatever capacity to get to Berty, I never told them the full story of course – I just told them what they needed to know. I kept the real reasons to myself; I didn't want them to decline my offer. Anyway I eventually got to the S.O.E. (Special Operations Executive) people and was offered the opportunity to

train. Once trained, I would be re-assessed and then maybe I would become operational."

Murtyl continued, "I had to undergo tests and training programs which were difficult for some of the highly trained officers – and even they failed some of them – but I passed them all with flying colours. They put me through hell and back." Murtyl started to smile, thinking of the things she had to go through, "It was a crazy time, I would have done anything to find Berty and that was only the start, the worst was yet to come. We were trained in camouflage, detection, evasion, hand to hand combat, (in which I had an advantage.) We also did safe cracking and breaking, burglary, how to survive in different terrains, how to blend in and go un-noticed in almost any situation. We were given exercises at training camps - we could be dropped somewhere in the country with no money and told to get back in the shortest possible time." Murtyl gulped a few sips more of her cold tea down. "The trouble was you had no ID papers, money or food rations. I was only beaten once by a guy, I later found out had been dropped in an area he knew really well. He had stayed with an old University mate, who gave him some really good food, then he gave the cheating bugger a lift back to the training camp gates."

Murtyl yawned, "I'm sorry, I am going have to go to bed now, up early for tomorrow!" Nick looked over at her wiping his eyes, "Okay Murtyl! Don't let me keep you; I have some errands to run tomorrow so I will have to be off at 5:30am, I hope this is not a problem?" As Murtyl stood up to go to upstairs to bed she smiled at Nick and replied, "No problem at all, go as you please. Hope you get some sleep, sweet dreams!" They both headed for their beds, Nick's head was racing with all the information that had been crammed into his brain that evening – he was so happy that Murtyl trusted him enough to open up to him and was looking forward to hearing some more.

4:30am soon arrived, Nick's alarm woke him up, he had slept well. Rubbing his eyes and stretching, he sprung out of bed and made his way to the bathroom to wash his face and brush his teeth. Walking back to his bedroom, he noticed that Murtyl's bedroom door was open and the bed was made. He smiled to himself at how organised she was and went to get dressed ready to face the day. It was a cold morning so he was pleased he had packed his fleece and extra vests to layer up, he looked through the window as he passed it to walk down the stairs, and noticed that there was a robin on the tree outside of the house – he knew winter was on its way and knew he wouldn't see Murtyl as much once the bad weather started as it was too dangerous to travel on the bike. He rushed downstairs to see what she was up to but she wasn't there, there was a note on the table, Nick picked this up, it read: 'Sorry to abandon you , I had a few jobs to do too. I will be back this afternoon if you are about. Drive safe – M. Ps. Hope you're layered up; it is cold out!"

When Nick got home, he returned to his normal routines and work. He tinkered with his race bike but always had Murtyl's life in the back of his mind. He kept asking himself questions like: What the hell had she been into and really done in her life? She is full of common sense, can poach, rebuild, build, shoot, drive, and ride with the best of them. She was like some sort of machine - what the blinking heck was she? Questions were running through his head - who really knows her, or more precisely, why does nobody really know or visit her? The Hardy's, Webby and all the people he knew through racing, he couldn't talk to. There was no way to research anything either Nick had already spent time in the libraries looking at newspapers to see if

62

there was any references to any of the stories Murtyl had told him about – not because he thought she was lying but because he wanted to go into more in depth and see what she was really up to. He soon realised he was not going to find anything and the whole thing was pointless. But he knew he had met the most direct, knowledgeable, bright, intelligent, pretty woman in his whole life. He just hoped that in the future he would meet a girl that had half of Murtyl's poise and attributes and if he did, he knew he would be a lucky man!

Nick carried on learning more from Murtyl when they had their ride-outs, drive outs or were doing maintenance. He even spoke to her over coffee, dinner or out shooting and poaching. Nick knew he had to get as much information from Murtyl as possible whenever she was talking and while she was about. He learnt so much about how to handle himself and about life as well as his own unexplored abilities, but there was rarely any more stories about Murtyl's life. It was becoming a really big problem with Nick's boss and to be honest it meant there would be no job soon. This was a real worry for Nick, he could not approach Murtyl with his problem, it would not be the honourable thing to do. All he wanted to know was how and when would she trust him enough to at least give him something more to go on.

Nick had a heavy night out with his mates and although he had suggested to Murtyl he would visit on the Saturday, he just was not in the mood. Neither had a telephone so he just left it and thought he would ride across to Hutton Rudby on the Sunday. Feeling a little guilty he slept badly on Saturday night, so got up and off quickly in the morning - he arrived in an hour. Nick quickly parked up, knocked on her front door to his surprise there was no answer. After a short while he went round the back, asking Steve, the Chef of the

Wheatsheaf, if he had seen Murtyl about. He said he hadn't! Once round the back he saw the garage was locked up as well as the back door, Nick was getting rather worried about her now. He knocked loud enough to wake the dead she must be up! Hell, it was after 0900hrs! After no joy at the house, Nick walked up to the shop and looked around, but she wasn't there either. Coming back down the village over the green, he noticed the lounge curtains were closed, he froze for a moment – his eyes were on stalks by this point. He knew there was something definitely wrong. He ran back towards the house noticing that the bedroom curtains were open but not the lounge. This may have been something and nothing for some people but not Murtyl, it was tardy and not like her at all. Nick began to feel really concerned but didn't really know what to do. He knocked again but to no avail. He spied down the edge of the curtains and could just make out there was a light on, this really caused him to panic and he could feel adrenalin flowing through his body, but he still didn't know what to do.

Instinct took over, his stomach churned, and he knew there was no time to waste. He went through the front door - literally! He had hit it hard with his shoulder a few times with no result, but he knew he had to get in, so bugger it, and rode his Kawasaki straight through her front door. He wasn't worried about the bike at this point; it could be fixed later. He dragged his bike back out, kicked the rest of the door in and rushed into the house.

Nick called her name and there was no reply - nothing at all. He knew she could sometimes be in her own little world singing to herself as she pottered about the house, but he still felt that something was very wrong. Nick turned right into the lounge and clocked the settee; he dropped to his knees and started to cry.

64

Murtyl was peacefully laid on the red settee in her best blouse and skirt, reading glasses on with a letter over her chest. Once he had gathered his composure Nick went over, knowing she had left sometime yesterday, as she was cold. He gently took the letter and read it through his watering eyes. It was from the Monastery in western France, it read:

Dear M,

It is with great regret I have to inform you that your great friend Albert Noir has passed away. He left peacefully in his sleep.

Please accept our deepest sympathy and understand that if there is anything you want from his belongings or records, it is yours. We understand he has no living relatives or associations with anybody except yourself.

All details and diaries will be forwarded to yourself in the next few days.

He has been a great asset to all who dwell here, and we do understand the two of you worked extremely well together.

If you could visit once more, we all choose to see you, thank you and bless you.

Please send no more financial assistance, Albert has only ever been an asset to us as you have been.

Bless you,
Charles Andrew Stuart Hobson.
As ever CASH to you.

P.S. I found this note from Berty.

Murtyl, My dear sweetheart.
I have just recovered from a stroke
and lost the use of my left arm.
I can never apologise enough for what
I have put you through now I have
been re-joined to my feelings.
The blockage of blood flow to parts
of my brain must have caused an increase in pressure elsewhere within
the cortex. The result is, I now remember!
I have failed you in the most important area of life. I know you loved
me, but I was unable to feel or to
know what love is. I have no excuse;
I know Charles and yourself did
everything you could to help me. Except bang me on the bloody head!
All my emotional faculties have been
reborn.

My dear I love you, with all my
heart. Please accept my deepest apo-
logies, and know, as I leave shortly,
I will be with you forever to support
and protect you in every way, every
day.

All my Love,
Berty.
X

He read through them again and began to understand
some of what must have taken place.

Nick surmised she must have received the letter late
yesterday morning and sat down to read it in the evening. Once comprehending the contents, grief and sad-
ness must have taken over as she lay there, and she
must have left as her will to live subsided. The medical
definition would be for a coroner, at the moment he just
needed to call the authorities.

Nick went upstairs and acquired a blanket, came back
down and gently placed it over this wonderful lady.
Leaving the house he secured the front door in the best
way he could and went to see Jo. He used the telephone
and called the Police. When this was done, Nick sat
outside Murtyl's front door with his head in his hands
for a few moments. He then pulled himself together and
waited for the Police to take over, to do whatever they
had to do. Nick had replaced the letter on her chest,
then ran over and over it in his mind wondering how
she must have felt whilst all the time regretting the fact
that he had not bothered to visit her yesterday. Nick
cried once more and felt so guilty.

Once the Police arrived, Nick gave a statement then was asked to leave, there was nothing he could do. They would arrange for the property to be secured and all the services to be cut off. The rest would be up to the Coroner, if they wanted to talk to Nick, they had his address. He went home pretty damn well unhappy with himself, the situation, and his guilt. His mind was filtering through every word in the letters; he was going over and over it in his head. Nick knew he had to get home as soon as possible because he was in no fit state to be on the road. His dearest friend and mentor had died, he felt a huge void. Nick knew he would miss Murtyl's presence in his life dearly.

The weekend dragged, it felt like time was standing still, he was in a nightmare state. Every minute felt like hours, and Nick's head felt like it could explode at any point. He was back into the office dragging his feet, the first thing Nick felt he had to do was tell his boss. This was done and he was told to take a few days off and dig into everything, as there was a story there, and he didn't seem to have it. Nick did as he was told and went home. Looking through his notes there was nothing he could go on, no facts that were provable, just her word which he totally believed in. Nick, however, had no proof of the life she may have led, he was in a situation now, as he didn't know what the hell he was to do. After the few days he went back and fronted up, he spoke the truth to his boss Bill. "I have nothing sir. I know what she did tell me, I know what she showed me she could do, but I have no way of putting all these things into the context of her life. I know about Mr. Noir in France, but he has died too." The answer Nick got in return did not surprise him in the least, his boss was not very sympathetic. "You know where the door is, and you must have some leads to chase up. You either have something or you don't. Your P45 will be here to pick up in fourteen days. I've had enough of the long leash I gave you!" Nick sighed, he had had enough of all the aggravation he was getting, and decided he wasn't bothered anymore. He walked out of the door and closed it behind him, he didn't feel like arguing at the moment and he certainly wasn't in the mood to be locked up for damaging property – so he left in silence, without a fuss, like he had never been there, shoulders sagging with the weight of emotion and depression.

Nick left the office and couldn't be bothered to empty the few things out of his desk drawers. He shrugged his shoulders and forgot about it, to him at the moment, life might as well be over. He kept his word to Murtyl and never said a thing to anyone about anything she told him. Bugger, he was in a hole, Nick knew it wouldn't take three weeks before he'd have to go back to his parents with his tail between his legs. He knew this whole thing was just impossible. Nick started suffering from depression. He stayed in his flat for a few days; he didn't get dressed, shaved, or washed. He tried to think of a way to walk forward with it all. He decided he would call the police in an effort to at least do something. The sergeant answered the phone, "I'm sorry son; there is nothing you can do at the moment. You are just going to have to leave it with us!" The police wanted another statement and then Murtyl's solicitor would arrange the house clearance once the coroner was satisfied. Until then, unless he was needed sooner, Nick had to just sit there and twiddle his thumbs. The Police never called.

Nick seemed to lose track of time, he suddenly realised that he was doing something Murtyl had never done and was letting his life waste away whilst he moped about something he couldn't change. He had a long shower, had a nice clean shave, and made himself look presentable. Running over to the calendar, Nick saw he had missed the coroners hearing and the next thing was the funeral. He was incredibly nervous and sad at the same time.

The 20th January arrived and sure enough, out of respect and love, Nick got to the service; he thought only he and one or two others would be there. Jobless and not too enthusiastic about life, he sat there in silence. His thoughts and feelings were all over the place. He started watching mysterious people arriving in limousines and entering the Church where Murtyl lay. They were all in suits - very flashy suits at that, and they seemed to come in pairs. There was no pattern to the pairs, some males, some male and female and some just females. Nick now had more questions running through his head; who the hell are these people? Why are they at my dearest friend's funeral? Why does he not know of them and why did Murtyl never speak of them? What did they want? After frowning for a few moments and getting angry at the thought of someone taking all Murtyl's assets from her, he realised that these people were from governments - diplomat types, as they seemed to wear, 'that kind of cut' of clothing. Nick then noticed they were different nationalities; he could tell as each pair talked to each other and acknowledged other pairs. This was really odd, so much so, he watched and listened. The service was short, it seemed to be over before it started really and then the body was taken to the crematorium, but nobody was supposed to go. Murtyl's ashes would be with her true love, but the whereabouts of that was not to be told. Nick really was getting his head into a spin at this; surely there was no issue in knowing where her ashes were to lie. Why couldn't he go and see them together just once to say his final goodbyes to his friend? Nick remembered Murtyl telling him about where Albert was and the name of the Monastery.

70

As the procession of people left after showing their respect, most of them laid wreaths by the door. They were all beautiful, most were small, but the cards nearly all read the same way. There was a national flag, a year or two years named and a very simple message in their own language. Nick made a note of what was on the cards to translate them later, they read:

"The freedom and stability of our nation can partly and directly be attributed to the action you took on our behalf. We will, as people, forever be in your debt. Thank you."

Nick's mind was just in a blur, he tried to talk to some of the mysterious pairs about the cards, but he was just ignored. He saw his boss who just shrugged his shoulders, as if to say, now can see what you could have uncovered, yet you failed. Nick didn't know whether to be angry or whether to cry at this point. He was in such a state, his motivation was none existent and Murtyl wasn't there to help him through the rough times ahead.

Nick left the service more confused than ever and the depression just kept deepening. No job meant the bikes had to be sold, the flat had gone, and this meant he had no bed of his own. All that there was for him to do, was to 'sign on,' then to start looking for jobs – fast!

Nick went for interviews; knocked on doors, offered to work for nothing for a month to prove he was good enough. The answers were all the same: 'We can't insure you to do that, you have no experience' the list goes on; it was all just a big nightmare. To top it all off, the girlfriend he thought he had, decided to leave too - was life worth bothering with? Life just all kept spiralling in on itself. People, Nick had known for

71

years, even from school looked at him as if he was a stranger. He had lost weight, aged, and his skin had a grey pallor to it, he really was in a state. Nick's family didn't really bother with him, they got on with their lives and just ignored his health and wellbeing - not even offering to help by listening. Nick started to clean windows and cut grass for people in the neighbour-hood, not taking payment, even when they offered – he did it just to stay sane.

After around four months a letter arrived through the letterbox, it had bounced around a few addresses, in-cluding his ex-employers, and eventually arrived at his mother's home. Nick opened it; after all it was ad-dressed to him. It seemed to be from a solicitors in Yarm. Yarm was a market town nearby to Hutton Rudby and not that far from Guisborough where he was now staying with his mother. Nick unfolded the letter and started to scan through it. What on earth had he got wrong now he wondered? It read:

Dear Mr. Nick ………. Would you please contact us and make an appointment with Mr. Ron Kirk as soon as possible."

Nick found the contact number at the bottom of the let-ter and gave him a call straight away. The following week was as soon as Mr. Kirk was going to be avail-able. Mr. Kirk would not disclose any information to Nick over the phone and said he would only release information in person. If Nick wanted to know what the solicitors had contacted him for, he would have to make an appointment and visit - so he did.

Wearing the best suit he had and borrowing his moth-er's car, Nick travelled to Yarm looking for the solicit-or's offices. It didn't take him long; he soon found them close to the market centre and he entered the gleaming

72

white building. Nick walked over some really thick
carpet and saw some eyes peering at him, he asked for
Mr. Kirk at the reception desk. He was beckoned to go
and sit down and wait while wondering what this was
all about. Once Mr. Kirk had finished speaking to his
last client, Nick was asked to enter his office. The office was plush with an old fashioned green light on a
large dark oak desk with a green leather inlay. The carpet was deep and in Nick's opinion was far too good for
an office – his mother didn't even have this sort of
quality carpet at home, never mind in an office. The
walls were hidden with deep dark bookcases full of
legal books and there were a few files on the floor.
Nick shook Mr. Kirk's hand and saw that he was a
pleasant, smiling, happy sort of chap. Mr. Kirk was
slight of build, he had grey hair - side parted and wore
gold rimmed glasses. The most interesting thing was
that he seemed to be happy, always smiling - Nick just
was not quite sure how to take this. The whole unem-
ployment, no future, down and out things were really
taking their toll and what the hell had he done wrong
now? Nick was offered coffee and asked several question about himself; date of birth, where he used to live
and what the registration was of the GPZ 550 that he
had sold. He proffered this information then he was
told that this was to do with a promise he had made.
Nick at this point raised his voice slightly, "I never go
back on my word and if I owe someone some money, it
will be paid back as soon as I can find work Mr. Kirk!"
Nick started to get worried, whom did he owe money
to? He couldn't put a name to any person; he thought
he was debt free. Mr. Kirk piped up, "Settle and relax,
this is nothing to do with you owing money, I have
been asked to do this on behalf of a client as their last
wish and I just had to be sure I was talking to the correct person. I am now satisfied and will get on with
business" Nick look confused and then looked over in
the direction Mr. Kirk was heading, what the hell was

he up to?

Mr. Kirk then pulled some papers from the safe hidden behind him and gently placed them on his desk. He spoke in a soft tone but a serious one, "This, young man is a contract between the deceased and you. The firm I represent, is working on behalf of the deceased, and will oversee this contract to its fruition. This maybe after I pass away, but the responsibility will be handed on to another partner within the firm until it is fulfilled. Would you sign here please? My secretary will witness it." Nick was about to respond when Mr. Kirk went back to his safe and pulled out a pile of diaries. Nick was then mesmerised and stuttered, "T-they aren't M-Murtyl's diaries, are they?" Mr. Kirk smiled; "You get this one to look at for three minutes, it is dated June 1944 to October 1945. It should, if you're as bright as I am told you are, give you a chance to read quite a lot of this." Nick took the diary with both hands and glanced at the first ten pages and burst into tears, handing the diary back to Mr. Kirk. He handed Nick a tissue and then spoke, "My name is Ron and I'm here to help you with this, but you have to make the decision regarding your word to this lady." Nick replied straight away without thinking, "Of course I want to write up that wonderful lady's life, she told me so much and yet at the same time it all seemed to be a fantasy. The only thing that was concrete were the skills she purveyed, the pictures on the walls and her car and bike, but the things she told me we're just hinting at something I know nothing of." Ron replied, "Yes Nick but it is all in her diaries! I can help you do the research you will need to do, as time passes more information will become common knowledge and it will get easier. The bones are in the diaries, but you can't have them without the contract being signed. Even then you will only get one at a time, as they must be followed progressively, and by her instruction. My instructions are

74

to keep this formally informal and to be by your side as and when required; help you with any legal issues and give you clear advice regarding time issues where the Official Secrets Act is concerned." Well that was Nick hooked, "If you are able, and have been instructed, then I have to do it, for Murtyl!" Ron smiled while handing the ink pen over to Nick, "Just sign here!" Nick took the pen carefully, it felt like a light had come on in the very dark life he was currently living, he signed on the dotted line very neatly considering his hand was shaking, and asked Ron another question, "What happens next sir? Do I get to take the first one home with me?" "No Nick you do not, there are other things to deal with first."

Ron's secretary witnessed the signature and left the room quickly before anything was mentioned. Ron was the first to speak, "Right Nick, your living situation is not really satisfactory at present and I need to know where you are and what you're doing, so you will be needing these." As Ron bent down towards a drawer he was opening, he held up some keys and handed them to Nick. "What are these for?" Nick asked.
"They are for our friend Murtyl's home, you are to use the house until you no longer need to, you cannot sell any of the contents, but you may replace and refurbish as required. I know your present financial position and to help you cope there is enough provision to cover the rates, poll tax and all utilities for eighteen months. Again I repeat you may never borrow against the property and upon your death it goes back into her estate. Murtyl believed this would be enough for you to have a chance in life. She was concerned she had compromised the start you had made, while she was assessing your trust worthiness and abilities to do as she has asked." Nick by this time was too dumbstruck to speak or move. After few seconds he looked up at Mr Kirk, his eyes were full of tears. His nose had started to run

too, as he tried to pull himself together. Just as he thought he had it all under control and attempted to get some words of gratitude with humility, his stomach started to tighten. Still shaking, he leant forward desperately searched for the waste-paper basket. He saw it, he really did do his best to get there, but the stomach muscles beat him, they wretched uncontrollably. The contents of his stomach rose with such enthusiasm, flying right over the top and passed by the basket. The second wretch he was ready for and targeted it well. Mr Kirk stayed calm behind his desk, not too sure if he was surprised by the emotional release the young lad was experiencing, or how his cleaners were going to get that stink out of his office. Obviously as a solicitor he knew the cleaning was chargeable to Murtyl's estate, but he thought that maybe just a little harsh to the great lady. On the other hand, he now knew she had chosen this boy well.

Ron ushered him outside and assisted Nick to his mother's car, "Relax Nick, take a few deep breaths and let it all sink in before you drive the car home. I expect you to be in your new home within a week and I want to see you here in two weeks' time, at the same time as you arrived today. I know there are some time issues with some of this stuff, so we need to be careful about how quickly or slowly, each of the diaries maybe worked upon. Most importantly we need to find you secure work as your confidence has taken a battering and I know you need to be at your best for this task."

After approaching the matter as delicately as possible with his mother, Nick moved to Murtyl's home with all haste. Settling in very quickly was not too difficult, he knew the property and its surroundings. Many of the villagers were only too happy to see him and in truth were relieved that someone they knew and trusted was going to be the custodian of the great lady's home, rather than any outsider, or for that matter Tom, Dick or Harry moving in. They realised that Murtyl must have had a great respect for Nick and that was good enough for them.

Nick, once settled as best he could, carried on looking hard for employment. He understood there were time constraints and any time wasted now could prove to be disastrous later. Fourteen days after he had last seen Mr Kirk he was back at his office as requested.
The day was agreeable for walking so Nick walked the six plus miles to the solicitor's office. It was just a few more pennies not being spent, which had to be a good thing. Mr Kirk (now known to Nick as Ron), very kindly befriended him, understanding how hard work was to find. While Nick was applying for work, Ron very kindly paid him to do some filling, painting of the premises and delivery work, just to help keep Nick's funds and spirits up.

After several weeks, Ron took Nick to one side for a little chat. "I can see why Murtyl had a soft spot for you. You just don't give up do you? Whatever is laid on you plate you take a deep breath, put your head down and grind on!"
"I try Ron, I really do try!" Nick answered as he put down the tools he was working with.
Ron raised his left hand and held it horizontally while bring his right up to slap into the left hand. Nick had not seen an object in Ron's right hand, but he did see an object leave it. It rose high and flew in his direction. Nick rose to catch it not knowing what it could be. It turned out to be a small black velvet bag with some-thing metal inside. Nick looked at Ron quizzically and Ron just smiled and opened his palms out toward Nick, as if to say open it.
Inside were two small keys on a metal key ring and a small leather patch. Still puzzled, he carried on looking

at Ron who said in his clear distinctive way. "The keys to the garage and the motorcycle. You need transport, I have insured it for you, and I know you won't be racing it. Look after it for her. I realise it is what you need, and she would approve!" Nick as ever, was humbled by her generosity. "Another thing Nick, you better have these ones too. You're not insured to drive her, but I know it would break Murtyl's heart if the Healy was not at least turned over and run up regularly, as well as being maintained!" Nick smiled at Ron, "I understand sir!"

Over the next few years Nick found good solid work and was fortunate enough to settle down with a lady – Heather, who to him was sublime. He had bumped into this lady - whose eyes had shone brightly into his soul. He wasn't mesmerised by her, he just knew the moment he saw her, his whole being had lifted and enhanced. They became best friends and inseparable. They played and worked together having a mutual understanding this would always be so. His smile, his stance and attitude displayed to all around his gratitude and happiness at being aware of their love for each other. In fact he now began to understand some more of Murtyl's words: 'Being aware of being aware, be the best of the best and be humble.' Every time he woke and opened his eyes, seeing her made his heart miss a beat as exhilaration ran the length of his spine and his whole body tingled with joy - with a happiness and eagerness for the day they would spend together. Whether it was at work or play, it did not matter. At every opportunity she would tease him, and he would tease her. The banter between them was never stale, it just exuded happiness. They spurred each other on to excel, they shared the same Mini and both raced it at different events and even occasionally, on two driver events, shared their stead. At home, servicing cleaning and set up was a shared duty. At the track he inwardly was always in wonder at how smooth and quick she was. He had read that the great Sir Stirling Moss's Sister, Pat Moss was actually quicker than he. Nick in his own mind, was witnessing this kind of skill now and did everything he could to find a sponsor. The only thing that did annoy him was that most days he woke up just before she did, which meant he got to make the morning tea and peppered toast just a little more often. Outside of that one duty, life was as perfect as he could ever have dreamt of - no jealousy, just absolute unwavering commitment to each other, and each other's dreams.

He stayed in touch with Ron and visited him often. They became good solid friends, meeting every few months for tea, coffee, buns, or cakes. Subjects of con- versations varied but usually came back to Nick's prosperity and the future. They never discussed diaries; it just seemed to Nick to be a taboo subject. It was just assumed by Nick that when the time came, he would receive the first one.

Chapter 8. The first Diary arrives by post.

A package arrived in the post nine years after Murtyl's demise, almost to the day. It was addressed to Nick from Ron Kirk.

He instinctively knew what it was, by its size, shape, and the senders name. Almost in shock, he wondered what this diary would hold. He took the package into the lounge and sat down on the great long red settee. Taking several deep breaths, he relaxed himself before slowly removing the string and brown paper packaging that protected the diary. Once all was removed, he looked at the cover of the dark grey A4 notebook with the marbled red print. On the cover it read 'First Tears' in her handwriting. He ran his fingers over these letters and stilled himself before opening it. As he did so, an envelope was freed and dropped out on to his lap. The envelope was addressed to himself; it was sealed, and his name had been scribed on the front by Murtyl. He lay back on the settee with the note, her diary on his chest and then he opened the letter. It read:

Dear Nick,

If you have this letter, then I have already had to leave one way or another. Ron Kirk will guide you through some things to keep you on the correct side of certain authorities.

The diaries are written post action. They are an outline, and you will, through research, have to verify a number of things. However I would like to explain why I have chosen you to take this task on.

I first met you in June 1967. I was the lady who arrived one night. Do you remember – I woke you up in your cabin on the super tanker 'SS Arabiya'? You were only four, we got on really well, and we tended to leave your older brother and sister to it.

In the few days I was onboard we struck up a friendship. Your Father - Cpt Nigel Pearson, accepted me onboard as I needed an escape route from the work I had been doing prior to the Suez Crisis. I am sure you remember a little! However, my exit route had been compromised, I was able to get to the SS Arabiya, as she was only 100 nautical miles away from the Suez entrance in the Mediterranean - half a day's steaming behind her sister ship. She was caught up in the crisis. You may recall our daily lifeboat drills and I used to point out to you various military things such as submarine periscopes, jets, and helicopters all around us.

After steaming up and down the Med, we were discharged in Sicily with your mother, brother, and sister, to fly to Rome and on to the U.K. Do you remember your brother being in trouble for dawdling and having chewing gum stuck to his short pants? Well I put it there to keep people's attention on him and away from me. You, bless you, took on the role of being my charge and we flew through all customs and immigration. Even at the tender age of four I became indebted to you.

I have watched you from a distance over the years and looked upon you as the child I never had. I have seen you racing in the Shell Oil championships with Geoff Towers, Alan Stewart, Dave Woolhams, and the rest. I have listened to their views on you and am proud to know of their respect for you.
This is why I have chosen you to do this for me; I know you will not let me down.

Be strong and be the best of the best, I will always be with you,

Love,
Murtyl.

For the first time Nick really began to understand and contemplate how much Murtyl had known and understood him. A few tears rolled down his face as the respect and love that he felt for her welled up within him. He placed the letter on his chest, and verbalised to the universe, "I won't let you down, Maaam." Then he closed his eyes and smiled to himself, as he relived the times he'd had with her.

After about half an hour, he brought himself back into the present, and opened the diary. He was to start learning about a whole new Murtyl.

First Tears:

In with the Baker Street Irregulars.

Interviewed by Vera Atkins for F section, (French section of the S.O.E.) The flat the interview took take place in was in Orchard Court, just off Baker Street in London's West End. All subsequent meetings and briefings were held there too.

I was never allowed into F section headquarters in Baker Street. I was greeted by Mr Park, who wore a dark suit and never asked names. He seemed to know all about myself and my past - I assume through MI5 and the mysterious Mr. Potter, they had done their research. I was escorted into the lift, through the gilded gates and taken up to the second floor. He would speak in perfect English or French, which ever was preferred or required by the occupant. He then ushered me into the flat and straight into the bathroom, which was used as the waiting room as no other space seemed to be available. The first time, waiting in the black and white tiled room, I was a bit nervy so I sat and relaxed as best I could on the edge of the black bath, and waited. Shortly after that Mr Park took me to meet Mr. Laurence Buckmaster - head of F section. He was slender, tall, and athletic, with thin fair hair. He was relaxed and introduced himself with a firm handshake. His only comment was, "We don't ask questions here!" With that remark I knew I had a chance. He then took off down the corridor with me in tow, and then turned into another room, introducing me to Miss Atkins. He explained that Miss Atkins would have all, or any dealings with me from now on, and she did. It would seem she had made up her mind regarding my recruitment within a few minutes of actually meeting me. We got on really well!

She even saw me personally to my plane for departure to France, after training.
I trained at the Thatched Barn under Capt. J. Edgar Wills in camouflage, coding and by some bloody magicians, to divert the eye while taking the prize. Hand-to-hand combat and assassination training was at Arisaig in Scotland. Unarmed combat training was with Willy Fairburn and Eric Sykes, who had been head of unarmed training for the Shanghai Municipal Police. They were brilliant but complete and utter bastards until they knew you were only going to play for keeps. Security and tradecraft was at B Group School at Beaulieu. Demolition techniques and wireless operations were at various country houses, and parachute training was with STS 51, at RAF Ringway just outside Manchester.

Chapter 9. Delivery of the parcel.

Four packages (myself being one of them) were laid up
for several nights in a safe house on the outskirts of
London. We were there for several nights and days
while we waited for a weather window so we could be
delivered. I was segregated while the other three were
allowed to communicate and build their cover stories
together. They were going to be delivered first and were
going to work loosely together all for the same network
within the S.O.E in Northern France. I was going in
alone to join and work for another network called
'Chestnut'.

When the weather was deemed to be good enough, we
were taken in two separate cars to an airfield. On arrival specialists trawled through all our belongings and
clothing with a fine tooth comb. Just the wrong kind of
polish or construction of shoe could be enough to have
you caught, tortured, and hung. They were good at it
and I was pleased they found nothing wrong with myself or my kit.

Going in alone, I had my own cover story to remember
and sort in my head. Vera Atkins - second in command
for the S.O.E. (F section) handed each of us a Cyanide
capsule, with a very solemn face, we all thanked her as
it now really sank home what we could be in for. Vera
then advised us she would see all our signals and work
as it arrived at HQ. She looked forward to both our return and debriefing us, she was always brilliantly positive and this I am sure gave us all confidence.

We boarded the four-engine bomber, a Sterling originally designed in America. It was 0125 hrs, and dark
with a moon that was no more than a quarter full. 161
Squadron flew these Sterling's, they specialised in this
sort of operation, dropping persons of counterintelli-

gence behind enemy lines and occasionally some pro-
paganda leaflets. On this occasion they had leaflets to
drop and three personnel, somewhere in the Normandy
or Brittany regions. They were dropped without incident, then we headed north west to drop myself at my
designated co-ordinance or reference point. This leg of
the journey would take an hour and a half.

With roughly 25 minutes to go, we were attacked. I'm
not sure what kind of aeroplane it was, probably an ME
110 night fighter that fell lucky on a lone allied aeroplane. Stirling's are quick when on full throttle and
could outrun most German aircraft but being caught at
a cruise speed of just under 200 knots meant we were
sitting ducks. The cover of darkness had not worked
out for us and we were strafed right along the fuselage.
The pilot threw her all over, climbing, diving, rolling in
a bid to evade our attacker. The airframe made stress
tearing and cracking sounds above the engines and
wind noise. The Pilot could not compete in this crate
with a fighter, but he tried bloody hard. The navigator
was strapped in, my handler, a sergeant and myself just
had to brace ourselves where we could within the fuselage. My parachute harness was unbearably tight and the
parachute behind me meant I couldn't get my backside
onto anything. I ended up lying on the floor with my
arms and legs spread out under the benches, wedged
into the sharp spars of the fuselage. The strapping
around my lower limbs (to protect my ankles as I was
jumping in shoes suitable for Paris life) was tight, making my legs and feet feel numb, like a block of wood,
which made it even harder to get that vital purchase on
the surfaces inside the violently moving aircraft. The
smell of fuel became quiet overpowering inside the fuselage, at least one fuel line or tank had been punctured. It took all my strength not to become a loose object clattering around the fuselage like a rag doll as the
pilot desperately carried on trying to evade our attacker.

The dark had to be on our side, the pilot just needed to find cloud cover, if only for just a few minutes. We had to be some-where north of the Central Massive, and there weren't too many fighter aircraft bases in that area. The Gerry couldn't have that much fuel; he would have to disengage at some point. We raced for cloud; the fighter had one last burst of cannon fire ripping through the Stirling, killing my handler. This final at-tack lasted a little longer, may be four seconds, his spent ammunition also went up through our cockpit. We started to climb hard; our angle of attack was too great, the engines started to lose their purchase on the air as we decelerated. The fighter pilot must have seen this and left the action, presumably to go and register his kill. The Stirling stalled, heeled slightly to starboard then started to dive. The engines began to scream as they were unable to keep up with the speed we were now gaining in the dive. I fell forward and took a few nasty knocks here and there, on the way toward the cockpit. A screen or two were blown out and the cock-pit was a bloody mess!

The Pilot and co-pilot had been slaughtered. The Nav-igator and I were left. I still don't even know if we had a rear gunner, never mind if the poor bugger had sur-vived or not. We hauled, what was left of the bodies out of their seats, I then took control. We were not in a spin, but we were rolling which made orientation relat-ively difficult. The Altimeter was reading just over 5000ft. I throttled back while feathering the props as she buffeted. My numb feet were on her rudder pedals and I started to try and pull her out of the dive, while rolling the yoke in the opposite direction to her roll, with a little left rudder. I screamed at the navigator to give me a hand on the other yoke. He may have only delayed for a few seconds prior to doing as instructed, but it seemed like an age as I fought and strained with

87

every ounce of strength I had. Eventually she responded and we started to bring her nose up. Once we started to gain height and we were out of the roll, the engines settled, and the propellers pitched correctly - we
started to climb steadily and safely. We had been as low
as twelve or thirteen hundred feet, so it had been pretty
touch and go. I could only hope we were still heading
in the right direction. The compass seemed to be
jammed on a heading, it did not move when I tapped it
and was U.S. Shouting at the navigator, I pointed to the
zip pocket in my jump suit that held out my field compass. The instrument panel had taken a few hits and
was in a state of disrepair. We had no oil pressure read-
ings, but the engines were still running, which was a
positive. We were losing fuel from an outer tank; I
made the relevant transfers to the inboard tanks and
locked the cocks off. Wiping blood off the other instruments and controls, I found we had airspeed, false
horizon, fuel, and the altimeter instrumentation only. I
didn't need to check the landing gear as I wouldn't
need it. The controls worked well enough, so the job
was still on!

I instructed the navigator - shouting as loud as I could
over the din, to find a heading for my drop zone. I intended to overshoot so that I would be able to turn the
Stirling round, head back over the drop zone and set her
on a vector and height that would get her and the navigator back over the U.K. If he was lucky. His name
turned out to be Bill, I could not describe him as it was
still dark, and we were running on infra-red light. He
was covered in blood as I was, in reality we were shadows to each other. I could say he looked terrified, but I
really didn't care. I shouted through the noise to look
on the bright side, he was alive and going home. He
looked at me oddly, wanting to ask the question 'HOW'
then he realised he was not going to be allowed to jump
with me and protested. I explained gently but firmly

88

that it would jeopardise my mission if he jumped and
was captured and I would happily shoot him if he carried on whining. I made a note of his squadron and I.D.
numbers as well as the name of his home-town. I then
proffered he would jump after I departed, so I explained
I would hunt him and his family down and dispatch
them on my return to England. At first there was an air
of 'you don't really mean that - you're a girl'. I held my
right hand up with the aeroplane's flare gun pointed at
him. I think all of a sudden he got the message that I
didn't care; I had a job to do and I am going to do it. If
you get in my way or cause me a problem, you die. He
now started to pay a little attention and began to focus,
realising his family and his survival depended on it.

I started to familiarise him with the instruments we had
left and the controls. At least as we were up in the air,
he didn't have to learn any take off procedures. I only
had to go through straight and level, using the bubble as
the false horizon, as it was still dark and there was no
horizon to work with. He was not as bright as one
would have hoped as a student, but maybe he felt under
a little pressure and was letting his nerves show - a bit
slack I thought! Once he got the grasp of four throttles
and was shown there was enough fuel to get home, he
started to sweat a little less. I gave him the yoke and
allowed him to get the hang of it, rotate clockwise, the
aircraft started to rotate clockwise, this caused slip and
so she began to lose height, rapidly falling to the right.
Enter a little left rudder, maintain the height, pull back
on the yoke and she would turn to the right. We prac-
ticed left and right turns several times and his nerves
really did start to settle. He started to chat incessantly
now - not something I have ever appreciated, never
mind under that level of noise while trying to teach an
idiot. We then went through throttle back, lose speed
and descend, throttle up, gain speed, and gain altitude.
The poor bugger was no natural, but we got enough

89

done in the half hour we had to give him a chance of getting home. The other option was to ditch in the Channel. I then had to go through engine shut down procedures and individual fuel cut off valves above the pilot's seat just in case he lost an engine or had a fire. If he were attacked, I just hoped he would have the decency to go down with her. He would only get one chance at landing, as I had no time to teach or practice go around procedures. On Sterlings, you had to remember that the flaps were operated electrically, but you could not do this at the same time as operating the bomb bay doors as they are on the same circuit. I didn't think that was too much of an issue as we were not on a bombing run and carried no explosives that needed to be jettisoned. Lastly, I had to go through descent routines and flaring close to the ground on landing, he would just have to use his own judgment and wing that one. At least he would he arrive over the U.K. as the sun rose. He would be able to see the ground and could use his eyes rather than go in on instruments alone. I then bid him tallyho, wished him the best of luck, and climbed out of the pilot's seat awkwardly. I moved to the rear of the aircraft, opened the door after I'd attached my static line and made sure it was secure. I then departed. The tail flew past my head as my static line became taught. I was rotating but not rolling as my parachute was deployed. As it opened my descent was only partially retarded. The canopy had not fully deployed, I kicked for all I was worth and eventually, about four hundred feet to go, she filled correctly with air. I smiled for the first time since leaving England, covered in blood, soaking with sweat, but soon I would be at work and about bloody time too!

My landing in the dark was a tad hard and solid. I rolled sideways as per my training and caught a rock with my left shoulder and the ground with my left elbow at the same time. The energy dispersed through my upper arm and there was a popping sound as the left shoulder was dislocated. It did smart considerably and was the first debilitating injury I had ever received in my life. So all in all this was not turning out to be one of the best days of my life so far!

I stood up and pulled my parachute in as best as I could with my good right arm, knowing I had to move. I was a good way off from the area my reception party should have been waiting. My concern now was: is there a different one waiting for me here after seeing my parachute and my damaged aircraft? Everything was collected up and I started to move as briskly as I could with the available moonlight. I needed to find shelter of some sort, a place to check my kit over, send a wireless message confirming I was on French soil and mobile.

After a mile or two, shelter was found in the form of a wooded area well away from any roads. My compass was in the Stirling on the way to England, so map reading was out of the question even when it was light. Finding a ditch located by a stream, I started to settle. Removing the flight gear and the wrapping from my legs, my body started to relax and breath. Thank the lord they fed us with steak and eggs prior to departure. If they had not, I would have been in trouble by now. Digging a hole to hide my parachute was too difficult with only one arm, so re-location of the shoulder became my first priority. The light was coming up as the sun rose, so I needed to look for a strong branch reaching out from a tree, a little below my shoulder height would do the trick. It took about ten minutes to find what I was looking for. I rolled up a glove and placed it in my mouth, then I lifted up my left arm over the branch with my right hand slowly and not without pain. Then I allowed my upper left arm to dangle over the thick branch. I moved my body closer to the branch

91

until my torso was an inch or so away from it and held my left upper arm with my right hand guiding the ball as close to its socket as possible. Once I was confident the ball was lined up to the socket as best I could, I then released the left upper arm and took hold of the left wrist with the right hand. I then dropped to my knees as quickly as gravity would allow, using my body weight to create pressure across the branch acting as a fulcrum, popping the ball back into its socket. My teeth clamped down on the glove, as I writhed on the floor for a few moments in a disturbing amount of pain. It would be sore, but I knew I was back in action. I waited a few minutes checking that all the fingers worked correctly on the left hand, there was no great smarting pain, and all worked reasonably well! Lucky, lucky, lucky - no trapped nerves, and the game was on. I washed in the stream, cleansing myself as best as possible - removing all that dried blood from the crew, then I rested in the wooded area - hiding until mid-afternoon. It was time to check through my kit, and try to get some bearings, then move!

As it happened when going through my kit, I found my transmitter was trashed, not from the landing but the shells that ripped through it in the aircraft. It was irreparable, the frequency crystals were smashed and there was nothing worth saving. This was something else that needed to be hidden, it meant there would be less to carry and less danger going through checkpoints, which was great, as they needed to be crossed. My paperwork was undamaged, which was great, I just had to hope they would be valid in the area I was now in. Luck could still be on my side yet! Everything I could lose was hidden and dug in as best I could, ready to move when the time was right.

As dusk started to fall, I started to move - heading west in the direction of the setting sun. I had exited the Stirling before we had reached my rendezvous point. The Sterling and Bill were heading home. Had Bill made it, or had the sod chickened out and jumped to save his own skin? He could have been captured and be giving the game away to the enemy right now - not a happy thought. The Nazis could be homing in on me right now, so I had to move and quickly!

I moved cross-country, looking for anything that would give me a clue as to where I was on the map. Sadly for me this part of France was quite flat - just rolling hill after rolling hill. When I came to roads, I followed them to junctions, but just as we had done back home, the direction signs had been taken away. I was going to have to take a risk or two to get a start. Hearing some approaching engines I took cover, they were twin cylinder Citroen's running on petrol, they had to be German. Hardly anybody in the country had access to petrol except the Germans. I hid, letting them pass and then I carried on.

Several more vehicles came by - one or two running on coke gas. They were slow and had to be French. Coke gas would allow an engine to run but it produced little power. If I played my cards right and kept up with this one, it would either take me to a village or at least a farmhouse. I was lucky as it turned out to be a farmhouse. I Observed from a distance through the night and then from dawn to dusk. This was done as it was unwise to approach until I was sure they had no guests from the military. Keeping an eye on the farm buildings, I made then my way to the chicken house and stole a few eggs. Still warm from the nest, I tapped them open one at a time on my teeth and swallowed the contents. I needed the protein. Carbs would have to wait for a less dangerous time. I then drank water from the cattle trough to quench a long arid thirst. I slowly moved onto the milk parlour roof where I could get a little sleep and observe my surroundings under the moonlight. Sure enough, the cattle in the fields started to queue at the gates near the dairy parlour at about 0430hrs. The farmer came out and started to perform his milking duties. The dozen or so cows took their turn for their teats to be wiped and allowed the farmer to squeeze from the top of each teat down over. The copious creamy milk flowed cleanly into the steel bucket before being transferred into milk churns. He was a large man; I would have described his as comfortable to cuddle up to as there were no bony bits. Once the cows had been milked, he cleaned out the byre and disappeared to tend to his other duties. This milk had to go somewhere and could provide my transport to the nearest village. It was safer to make no contact, than to make contact with a German sympathiser.

At around 1100hrs, a coke gas fuelled flatbed truck lumbered its way up to the farm. It was a rusty old Renault with a little blue paint still hanging on to parts of the cab. The driver got out of the old rust bucket, jumped down onto one leg and limped onto the other. He did not hobble badly and seemed to have a happy air about him. Weathered, and with tan coloured skin, he wore a washed out blue shirt with a red neckerchief wrapped around his neck and a British style flat cap. Probably in his forties, he really was so French it was funny.

The driver loaded the dozen or so churns the farmer had left out on to the Renault, he finished just as the chubby farmer returned. His sheep dog was clinging to his leg, desperate for the next command. His trousers came up to his chest and were held there with a big buckled wide brown leather belt. He wore wooden soled shoes and a cream vest. His head was almost bald and was full of smiles when he saw the Renault driver. They greeted each other and headed to the farmhouse.

94

The farmer's wife came to meet them, a bottle of wine in hand, some cheese, and a long loaf of bread she must have baked herself. She had grey hair tied up in a bun and was round faced with red cheeks. Her smile was as broad as it could be, competing with her backside, which was swaying in a large tie dyed green skirt. Her blouse was partially hidden under an old apron covered in flour.

They sat together enjoying their lunch and laughed as they did so at each other stories.

Slowly I moved to the blind side of the truck and opened the driver's door as quietly as possible, then I started to go through his paperwork. His next stop was Rebais. I retired to my hiding place and looked at my silk map. Rebais was about 30 miles north east of Paris. Bill had not done too bad a job of navigating, as I was about ten miles away from my original target. On the back of the Renault, a few wooden boxes were held in place by ropes attached to the cab. I now returned to the truck and checked inside them both, one was empty and the other was full of coke to use for fuel. This idea could be stupid and reckless, but I needed to find some sort of cover. With what was left of my kit, I climbed into the empty box and waited. Ten dusty minutes later the truck was started, and we were on the move. The truck dawdled along at a very sedate pace. I heard the driver shout to a few people as he passed them by telling them he had no time to stop as he had a rendez-vous for which he couldn't be late. A little later the truck pulled up, the driver disembarked and opened a gate into a meadow. He then drove the truck through and parked up in the meadow, closing the gate as all good country people do. Leaning against the truck I heard him fiddle around a little and strike a match. I could smell the smoke from his cigarette as he hummed a tune. I then heard the sound of a bell on a bicycle and a girl shouting the name Andres, to which he the driver

95

answered in a flamboyant manner to show his enthusiasm to see her. They laughed and joked a little, and then walked a little way into the meadow with a package I assumed must be food.

The sounds coming from the meadow made me giggle a little; they were having some real fun together - the kind you can only do with your clothes off! I didn't need to see any of it to know he was an experienced man. When they finished, they started to eat, talking about the aircraft that had gone over the night before. The Germans tracked the aircraft with radar after it had been attacked. They knew it had been hit and were trying to work out why it had come over this way but had headed back out on a completely different vector. They had not seen me jump from the aircraft. A local farmer had seen something, but he would not parley with the Germans. My mind was racing, could these two be sympathetic to the allies, I listened a while longer. They were exchanging information quietly and it was difficult to hear, but I did hear the phrases, fuse wire, and attack. It was time to make a decision: do I reveal myself and ask for help, or do I stay hidden and have no control of what may happen later? Both were high risk, but before I had thought through the dilemma, my body was out of the box and I was walking towards them in a military style.

Knife in one hand and pistol from my kit in the other, I approached the two who were making love again. I arrived at the top end so to speak, or at least where the heads were. She was face up, eyes shut, moaning while writhing in a rhythm that matched his. Her long auburn hair was gripped in his fists as he drew her towards him with each energetic thrust of his hips. His breathing became harder and faster - as was hers. I thought I'd best interrupt before they got to the point of no return! Tapping her in the shoulder with the knife and cocking the pistol in my right hand inches from his head, I said, "Andres" firmly but not too loudly. They froze, both looking up at myself in terror before they looked at each other. The sweat was beading off both their faces. He rolled over so they both laid naked in front of me. I glanced down and stated to the girl, "You're easily pleased I see!" They grabbed some clothes to place in front of themselves. I then asked, "Is there room for another?" That seemed to break the ice nicely and they burst out laughing. Quickly we got to grips with the fact they were not in the Resistance, but they did do a little courier work. To put me in contact with the Resistance would be difficult and it may take a little time, although between them they would hide me. This would mean meeting his wife and possibly her husband - they asked me to be discreet! I suggested we get on and discretion would be my pleasure, then laughed.

I was two days in hiding with the help of Andres and the girl, before I was picked up by two members of the Resistance. There was no need to blindfold me, as I was placed in the boot of their Citroen Traction Avant. This model of car was favoured by the Resistance, it had front wheel drive, it handled very well indeed and was easy to maintain. Access to the boot was from inside the car, which made security for the two men easy, and transporting me not too difficult. They were pretty rough with me, which was unpleasant with my slightly bruised shoulder. However I did appreciate their dilemma. Was I the real deal, the person that should have been with them four or so days ago or was I a German plant? I had no choice but to trust them, roll up in the boot and enjoy the ride. They had placed some blankets over me and instructed me not to make a sound no matter what. In the end we were never stopped by any checkpoints, which was great, but running through my mind was how had we not been stopped by any checkpoints and was I in the hands of the Germans? The car

97

pulled up and entered a dark garage via a ramp and I presumed doors. I was asked to get out of the car once it had stopped and noted the garage was dark inside. As I was exiting the car, my hands were tied behind my back and I was blind folded. I was feeling pretty rubbish to be honest; the journey had aggravated my left shoulder and the bruising was really coming out now. They bundled me around a bit then knocked me unconscious. Later, coming round I found myself tied to a chair still blind folded. It took some time for my mind to clear. For a short time I played a little, pretending not to have woken up. I wanted to know what I was in for, was I with the right people or had I really made a boo boo and was now captured by the Bosch.

As it happened, I could only hear the French language being spoken - a little comforting but I was by no means home and dry yet. I noticed there were no jack boots stomping around but this in reality did not tell me anything. The first thing that really hit me was the odour of the bloody place. This was no ordinary garage, yes there was the smell of leather, oil, and the usual petrol smells, but there was something else. Then it dawned on me and I got really quite excited, memories came flooding back in vivid colour with happy emotions. It could not be so, surely? Vera would have told me if MI5 & 6 had done their job properly. Yet no, maybe they had not put two and two together, I don't know, what I did know was I needed to hear two voices before I could be sure and let anybody know I was fully awake. The smell was from engines that had been pushed to the limit - that slightly burnt odour so distinctive to racers. Then two more men came in, a hot bright light shone into my face and the blind fold was ripped off. I blinked, screwing my eyes up, all I could see was the light. My interrogators were all stood behind the burning brilliant light. One man then came from behind me placing a pistol barrel to my head and

cocked the trigger. They were extremely serious and
wanted to be sure I was authentic, and not a German
plant. They knocked me about a little and really put
some effort into prodding my left shoulder - that did
smart, it was now well and truly black and swollen.
Tears were running down my face with the pain, as they
looked through all my clothes. It was only now that I
realised that the clothes I had been wearing were being
searched too. I was in my underwear only. Now I was
wondering what they would put me though next, then I
heard the tone, the commanding, distinctive voice of
the eagle beaked nosed, slicked back hair WW1 fighter
ace, and tears of pain became ones of joy as I started to
laugh. I shouted to Uncle Robert, "Is Willy here too?"
and everything fell silent. I shouted, "You haven't for-
gotten your favourite niece - the little girl you taught to
drive, fly, and race and bought her first car with Uncle
Willy, have you?"
Robert replied, "Mon Cheri, it can't be you, you can't
be the precocious little girl we love so much all grown
up, can you?"
"Oh yeeeehhhs, don't you recognise me?" The silent
Willy Grover Williams then stepped in and freed me.
He picked me up and cuddled me. Willy, Robert, and I
hugged each other, and we all leaked a lot from the
eyes. Later Willy told me it was the way I say Yeeehhhs
clinched it for him, I don't know why I say it that way
other than it is always good to question and my father
taught me that.

Uncle Willy then looked down at my shoulder and
winked, "OOOUUch, just a moment. Auntie Yvonne
makes just the stuff for that!" He came back a few moments later with a couple of small jars and started to
apply some to my exposed left shoulder. It was sore
anyway but with the bashing it had taken from my interrogators and the journey, it was particularly inflamed
and angry. Willy then started to speak to me in English

in his particularly calming soothing voice. I felt at home with these two gentlemen anyway, he revealed to me that his father was the famous horse racing trainer from Berkshire, and this was why his English was so reasonable. His mother was French, and he had grown up bi-lingual. His style was French - well dressed in a suit and tie, his hair slicked back on top of his oval face with a rounded but noble nose. His eyes smiled and I could see why Auntie Yvonne had fallen for him. Now he smiled at me, his face was full of mischief and he told me a few stories from before the war that I knew nothing of. He had been quite a tennis player and a lot of the other drivers had no real idea of who he was. He liked it that way! He had started as a chauffeur, and had gained an entry into the first Monaco Grand Prix in 1929 as a privateer in a borrowed Bugatti type 55, I think. Holding off those massive Nazi sponsored Mercedes, he won the race most unexpectedly. His tennis playing friends were gob smacked and now there is a museum to celebrate him in Monaco. He had been in France during the start of WW11 and done what he could to help the Allies. While the desperate escape from Dunkirk was being undertaken, he had driven a British General trapped behind the German lines through and up to St Malo, where they returned to the UK together.

He had been in England but a short while and was trying to find a way back to France, when he was recruited by the S.O.E. He did return to France but with the code name 'Vladimir' in 1942.

He was living above a tobacconist in Paris, his mission was a mixture: to help allied flyers evade capture and return home; to arrange air drops and build cadges of weapons for the future recruits; and to train fellow collaborators in sabotage and as "Sir Churchill' had said, 'Set Europe a light!' He did this with enthusiasm and built up an organisation called Chestnut. During this

100

period, his wife was not aware he was back in France as it was in his opinion too dangerous for her to know. It was during this period he recruited his racing team-mate Robert Benoist into the Resistance network to work alongside him.

He then made me laugh by telling me stories. These were ones such as: He and Yvonne used to drive around Monaco in separate cars. He would lead and she would try and keep up as they raced around when there was no actual Grand Prix on. Occasionally she would be stopped by the Police for driving too fast, to which she was always damned annoyed. She would complain, "There are no speed limits so what is the problem and I'm only trying to keep up with my husband!" The answer would come in reply, "I am sorry ma'am, we do not stop the great Willy."

The bruising in my shoulder was calming down now, and they suggested I should try to have a night's rest. For now it safest to stay in the garage, at least until we or they had come up with a plan for us to walk forward with. I bedded down on a chaise lounge in Robert's office. They laid blankets over me, and I drifted away feeling safe, warm, and secure for the first time in five or so days. It was good to know they are there, and I was safe for now.

The next morning came and they both arrived with cheese and baguettes: 'pout le petit de-jonais'. We ate and Will looked at my shoulder. It was still sore and a little stiff, but the bruising had all but disappeared. Willy produced another cream, saying this one would tighten the ligaments up in a few days. Then and only then, would they allow me to start moving my shoulder to get my mobility back. The three of us discussed my future; they were very intent on my returning to England as they knew the dangers and probable longevity

101

of a new S.O.E. agent in France. The Jerries were improving at catching spies and the average survival time was less than a few weeks. The two of them really were intent on sending me straight back to Blighty. They were never going to let me win the argument and, in the end, I then told them about Albert and they both leant back in their chairs and whistled. "You crazy girl, we just told you how dangerous it is to be here. You cannot work with us, you know why. Now you tell us the truth, this is not a game. Those bastards out there play for real; do you understand?" questioned Robert.

I replied, "You have no idea how bloody hard it has been to get here. You have no bloody idea how easy I find it to kill, and you have no idea what I am prepared to do to get to him. With or without your help, I will play my part in this sodding war. Don't even try to stop me, be with me if you choose, but I beg you, not to be against me." They retired for ten or fifteen minutes, returning with a compromise. Willy spoke first.

"Sweetheart, it is with such a heavy heart we cannot allow you to work with us here. We understand your conviction and know how stubborn you always have been, so we have a suggestion that we think may work for you, and we can cope with."

I replied, "I'm listening!" Willy then explained their plan and I took it all in. We discussed how I would contact them, that I would be working alone, I must always stay on the move, never staying in one place more than a day or so to reduce the risk of capture. They would answer my coded letters, through BBC broadcasts, confirming or refusing help with operations. They would courier money to me occasionally or to prearranged drops which we would work out there and then. Once this was all agreed, they would get me out of Paris as soon as possible with the correct clothing and passes to start my search and new career. I was chuffed with my negotiating skills and knew it was going to be O.K. as long as I got off on the right foot.

As we all relaxed, knowing we had agreed a way to move forward, I asked, "Where is Jean Pierre, why is he not here with you both?" Jean Pierre Wimille had been Uncle Robert's teammate and protégé - driving for 'Ettoire Bugatti' and the works Bugatti team just before the outbreak of WW11. Jean Pierre had been in a horrific accident just before the war and was starting to make his comeback as it all became a little thick. In 1933 Jean Pierre had been asked to join the Bugatti team as a test driver and later became a works competitor. His best achievement with Robert was winning the 24 hrs Le Mans in 1937 and 39. At this particular time, all they knew was he had been designing cars to suit the public pocket post war, in the hope he would be able to build them after the war. What my two heroes did not know was, Jean Pierre was also in the sabotage game and not that far away! Over the next few days we worked together on our future communication systems and codes. I was allowed to rest my shoulder. With the help of Willy's creams my ligaments tightened quickly, and it was only three days before I had full movement and strength back, although it was still a little sore. They had gone out and bought some beautifully designed clothes for me. I laughed when I saw them and said in an incredulous way, "You bloody idiots, what the hell good are these fantastic clothes to me? I mean they are fantastic, but when am I going to get to use dinner dresses, patent leather shoes and/or coats and hats. They must be black market, or have cost a small fortune, and sadly I wonder if they may have alerted the Bosch to something!" Willy and Robert just looked at each other almost in a state of shock and dismay. Willy spoke first, with his soft soothing tones.
"My little love, what have we done wrong for you? You are elegant, beautiful and you ooze style and confidence. Neither of us can ever see you in any other than the most luxurious, designer clothing. The clothing you

103

arrived in has been destroyed and this is who you are now you have grown up - to Robert and me at least. I think you have caused us to forget about the war!"

"Oh shut up, you two romantic idiots! Where am I going to go to dinner parties? It's not like it was before this war. Some parts of your life may not have changed like it has for others. All I know is there will be no parties in the near future for me. I know you can't take the stuff back, but I also know my Aunt's will take them, when you see them." I looked at them rather sternly I thought and then continued, "I need all the support I can get from you two at the moment." I sat in my favourite office chair within the underground Bugatti workshop on Avenue Foch in the centre of Paris. I carried on, "I have no clothes as you have burnt what I had. You want to dress me like a doll, and I am beginning to feel the need to thump the two of you! What I do need is a country skirt or two, some cheap blouses, a couple of pairs of trousers for working in the fields, some working/ walking style boots, and a good rain proof coat. The girly stuff is out, do you two damn well understand?"

Robert piped up, "I think we do; we were just so excited to see you and got carried away in the moment. Once the people on the black market could see we were spending, they were not shy to take the opportunity to pile more onto us. We do understand and will put that right today. Oh by the way, I can tell you that the navigator you sent back is in a bad way, but in the U.K. He will be O.K. He has asked for this message to be given to you. I quote 'Hope we never meet again, good luck.' I think maybe you have used your charms on him a little eh?"

"He's alive and at home, lucky, lucky boy!" I replied, as I smiled innocently toward him.

Once we had my attire right and had sorted my papers and passes out for my new role, we bade our goodbyes.

104

This was harder than I thought. I had no idea how much I loved these two guys. They were just the best and I really do mean some of the best men I was ever to know. Love oozed out of them - no wonder the crowds at the races and their fans cheered and loved them. They were just both unbelievably strong willed, caring, gentle warriors of the track, and now, thinking about it, that is what they had to be. Bless them, they took me to my first drop point, and we chatted all the way in a bloody great big Bugatti. The cheeky buggers drove up Avenue Foch towards the Arc de Triumph, right in front of the jerries' faces, so to speak. How they had the gall, I will just never understand. On route, they pointed out the SD and Gestapo HQ at No 84 and 85 Ave Foch, where the Nazis took captured spies and broke them down. They then carried on right through Paris. Before we were out of the true centre, we stopped at a most beautiful restaurant. We ate like royalty. The food was stupendous compared to the rations back in the UK - it was just fantastic. Nothing seemed to be on the menu and yet whatever these two heroes asked for just seemed to be possible and available for them. Willy asked me to memorise where we were, and the style of the buildings - but no names. He told me that the head waiter and owner had nothing to do with the Resistance and served Germans with good food. They had to make a living. However they were 100% trustworthy and were their friends. If I were ever in trouble and could get to either of those, they would keep me safe while they sent information to one of them. I understood exactly what they were telling me and committed the area and the portrait of the cafe to my mind.

After the most fantastic lunch I can really remember, we travelled out on the hot dusty roads past the outskirts of Paris and on into the country. They dropped me with a farmer whom they knew was safe. I was to stay at the farm for one night only and then move on.

The one thing I still had intact was the 90,000 francs Vera at the S.O.E. had supplied me with in a battered French suitcase. Money was no problem, but as I had to carry it, and it was cash, it would raise serious questions if I were stopped and searched. It was just another thing to be aware of and keep me on my toes…

After our goodbyes, hugs, kisses, and tears, as well as the promise of seeing each other soon, they both left in the flamboyant way that people do with a glass or two of wine inside them. My heart sank a little, but the farmer and his wife were grand and opened their arms and gave me hospitality like any great farm does. Their dog, a beautiful black Labrador bitch, slept the night with me, it felt as if I were her responsibility and I have to say, I liked it! She just lay by my side on the bed, her muzzle resting on the top of my thigh, just looking into my eyes until lights out, while I stroked her.

Chapter 10. Into the Unknown.

I awoke with the cockerels the next morning, feeling
pretty good. It was warm and bright outside; the air was
definitely fresh - if not a little farm like, if you know
what I mean.
I decided to go through all my kit again, just as had
been done pre-flight by the S.O.E. packer's, and then
by the best two uncles one could ever have. I tried to
relax. This was it - the big step into the unknown. I
really was on my own, no team to join and nobody or
organisation to meet. I really, really was on my own. It
was sinking in slowly how independent I was going to
have to be. My clothes were clean and were of local
manufacture, there was nothing that could give me
away. My footwear was correct, with my city shoes in
my bag and my papers which I was assured were good.
My pistol was in my pocket, a little spare ammunition
in my handbag and that cash was in my suitcase. Now I
had to go to my suggested starting point, going through
Metz and then onto Strasbourg. I knew Strasburg was
on the French-German border and Stuttgart was just a
little further east where the Boch had their Mercedes
Benz factory. My two Uncles had taken me as far as
Chalon en Champagne, which was about halfway to my
intended starting point. The farm I had stayed in
overnight was far enough away from them not to cause
either of us issues. I presume they had stayed somewhere else last night as they could not have returned
home before the curfew kicked in.

From here I made my way on to Metz and then back
towards Luxembourg. The papers my Uncles had
provided me with were now becoming less and less
effective. I just kept running the gauntlet across land,
hoping to get to the Rhine. That had to be my best way
up towards Switzerland and the area I was interested in.
Uncle Robert and Willy had given me enough Francs to

bribe my way through most things, as long as I kept my head. Even though I still had my case full of cash, they thought it better to have cash in my pockets and purse rather than delving into the suitcase. Their only instruction was to keep my head down and stay out of sight as best as I could. Whenever possible, I would travel cross-country slowly and by night. I bathed in troughs and streams, keeping my clothing as clean as possible. Hotels could not be used, but I did find the odd sympathetic farmer or two. Eventually, after two weeks on my own, I reached the Rhine and then I fell lucky. I had skirted round Ettelbruck, Diekirch and Tandel in Luxembourg avoiding contact with anybody and got to the Rhine. I really needed to bath properly after so long living off the land and, to all intents and purposes, was on the run, so I was feeling pretty grimy. I tried to cope with that dirty feeling, but in the end decided to take a risk. Hiding all my clothes and the few things I had in the reeds on the river back, I went for a swim. It was dusk - around 2230hrs. The water was crystal clear, cool, and soothing after the long hot day. It was just what I needed, and it felt fantastic. Without thinking, I allowed myself to drift out just a tad too far and was caught up in the current of the deeper water. It was too much for me to combat and I started to drift down stream. Slowly I lost sight of my hiding place and I knew it meant trouble. How the hell was I going to get back to my gear, in my birthday suit without any questions being asked?

I then heard the rapid thunk, thunk of a steam engine. Looking around, I saw rather large barge heading up stream toward me. It drew closer and closer. The river was too wide, and the surface was like a looking glass which made it impossible to make a swim for it - the German guards or lookouts on her would spot me instantly. The best I could hope for was to tread water and ride her bow wave once she was close enough to me.

108

Then I could escape to the shoreline using that latent energy. As the barge drew close, I realised how big she was - not like a British sixty footer, she was more like a 30,000 ton ship. Her beam had to be thirty to forty feet across. I needed to swim hard or be hit and pummelled to death. If I escaped that, the draw from her screw would pull me in and chop me up. I started to swim away like billy-oh. This inevitably disturbed the water's surface, and I was seen. There was no warning, high speed lead just started to crack down towards me from the soldier's rifles. A search light came on and I was going nowhere. I'd lasted two days and was bloody well caught! The barge was throttled back and started to slow down quickly traveling against the current. The power of the water moved me towards them, and I could do nothing about it. I treaded water and a line was hurled at me - it was a case of take it or be shot. Once the line was in my hands, I was drawn closer to the barge's side, and the soldiers began to realise I was female and in my birthday suit. They started to josh each other as to their catch and who would have me for dinner, while I was being hauled up the vessel's side to meet my captors. At that point, the Captain came out of the bridge and started to have a go at the six German guards. He stated that it was pretty unlikely that a slight girl with no cloths on could be too much of a threat to the mighty Third Reich. He offered to report them to their superiors and they reluctantly backed down. He and his mate hauled me in, took me on board and dried me off. Cpt Jan Lever and his engineer had come on deck to see what the commotion was about. They were both Dutch and the Captain introduced his engineer as Mr Jo Kendra.

About 0400 hrs, Cpt Jan Lever aroused me in my bunk and asked if he could have a little chat. He spoke in French, as I had only communicated in French during my capture. He wanted to know where I was from, why

109

I had a Parisian accent and how was it I had swam so far from my clothes. I answered this, knowing that telling the truth as far as possible, made it much harder to spot any miss information. My presumption was that the Guards were listening through the air vents of the cabin. The steel walls were painted dark green, on the bulk heads water was beading as the dew point had fallen in line with the ambient temperature. There were two bunks and a small table in the dank cabin. While we went through my story, I noticed his cap was partially on its side, resting on the back of the chair. I could just make it all out in the dim light that Captain Jan Lever was a stout chap, balding and portly, about five foot nine inches with a round face. He probably liked a beer or two as his face was a little red and ruddy, but that could be the outdoor life. His breath smelt of tobacco, but his smile was warm and friendly. His clothing was that of a man who was in charge of his vessel and crew. His pullover was high necked, and his trousers were moleskin, his unlit pipe hung from his unshaven jaw. Inside the cap I could see on the chair, I could just make out a faint and dirty piece of cloth that just may have been once in its life orange in colour. My mind raced, could he be on our side, and if so, how the hell could I make him give himself away? I talked away to him about needing a swim and a wash, then getting caught in the current, while thinking we must be miles upstream by now. I started to tap my finger on the bunk side, very slowly, gently, and very deliberately, I tapped the first verse of the Dutch National Anthem. Pausing, I then tapped out in morse code the Dutch King's name, then our King's name. I stopped to wait and hoped there would be some recognition. A tear slowly rolled away from his big blue left eye as he tried not to smile at me. He then lent forward and gave me a brief hug, whispering into my ear in English, "I understand, I and my crew are here for you, we will find a way." He then left.

110

I was locked in the steel cabin; my life was now in the hands of Cpt Jan Lever's and his crew. As ever my mind raced forward churning with thoughts. Would I be questioned in the morning? Undoubtably yes. Would I be turned over to the authorities or shot? There would be no sleep for the rest of that night!

I can only presume dawn broke, all I could hear was the engine of the barge pounding away, spinning her propeller, thrusting us forward up the Rhine. I had no idea of the time until the second in command - the engineer, came through the door with some pretty dire bread and hot broth which tasted of nothing, but it was food, and it was cooked. I still had a few rough blankets around me, and the crew had kept the German guards away from me through the night - things to be thankful for! The engineer introduced himself as Johan Kendrew. As he handed the bread and broth to me, I reached forward with both hands allowing my modesty to an extent to be exposed. He took his time but turned away slowly, after making an approving gesture with his lips. He then turned and took off his leather black cap, revealing a short back and sides haircut, he had a dirty neckerchief hanging around his neck underneath a grubby collarless shirt, and this was under a dark leather waist coat type of jacket. His sleeves were rolled up, bearing forearms caked in grease and coal dust. He was broad across the back and his greasy trousers came up above his waist, and halfway down his shins toward a pair of clogs worn with no socks, showing ankles caked with the same muck. He spoke in Dutch at first, I think, then he used a little French. I responded to the French and he turned to me as I bade him. His right hand moved towards his buttons just below the rope that acted as a belt holding those trousers up. As he did this, I readied myself as best I could for the forth coming rape attempt. I only had two blankets and the empty broth mug to use against him. Instantly I was ready in my

111

crouched position on top of the bunk bed. He seemed to sense my response and lifted his left arm. As he did so, I leaped forward and took his middle fingers in the palm of my right hand. Stepping forward, compressing the two fingers in on themselves towards his palm. I lifted my left hand allowing the mug to fall, as my right leg came round behind his calves. He began to buckle backwards with the pain in his left hand and fall over my right leg; I stepped around his back placing my left forearm across his neck. Releasing his hand as he fell into me, I went onto my left knee leaving the right one raised with the foot on the ground so that my foot was on the deck and my knee was bent at ninety degrees. My right hand was now behind his head and the left hand cupping into my right elbow while being wrapped around his neck. His own body weight would break his neck if he struggled. His hands dropped and he relaxed, then slowly his right hand rose up and I tightened my hold again. It moved slowly and deliberately towards the top of his trousers and then up a few inches to the same button as before on his pants. He turned the edge of his buttoned flies over, quite deliberately and slowly revealing a tiny button sewn on the reverse side of the flap. It seemed to be a spare button, he rubbed it a little to reveal it was orange. I immediately relaxed and helped him to his feet. He shook my hand and whispered "We are for you! I will find some clothing. This morning early, our guards were changed. They know from the other guards there is a French girl we caught in the river yesterday. They will not touch you as long as they think we use you. Please you must strike and cut my face. This will keep the cover for you until we make a plan." I smiled at him and let him leave with a loose tooth, and a light gauge just below his left eye. The same eye that would be black and very swollen just a few minutes later. He now left and the door was bolted behind him. Now it was just waiting game.

112

An hour or so later Johan came back, this time with a German guard. The Guard looked me up and down as Johan handed me some of his and Captain Jan's clothing. There were no shoes or clogs. The shirt I was given, I could get into twice, as I could with the heavy Hessian pants that were very rough. The Guard laughed at the state of me as I put these clothes on. However the garments were clean and dry. I must have looked like an orphan girl in grown up clothing. I think this caused the guard to think I was about thirteen years old or so, rather than my true age. He left shouting to his fellow guards that I was just a little child and to leave me to the crew for fun. I could be no danger to the Third Reich, there was no need to place me on the reports. Jo winked at me, then advised me that he would take the wheel and Cpt Jan Lever would be with me soon. Again the door was closed behind him, only this time it was not bolted. I waited and waited.

Cpt Jan Lever entered several hours later and advised me that the Guard shift would be changed again shortly. He suggested that within a day or two the German guards would not be aware I was there. He would somehow acquire some more suitable clothing and I would have to hide in plain view as a crew member and cook some of the rubbish they were all surviving on. All went to plan as we steamed further and further up the Rhine towards Switzerland. The trust between the three of us seemed to grow and after a few days we seemed to have gelled to an extent as a team.

When the opportunity arose, I hoped to find a way to explain to Cpt Jan that I needed to leave the vessel quietly and without being seen somewhere around the French, Swiss boarders. He wanted to know why I did not want to sit out the war with them on the barge. Their chances of survival were good, the Allies were

113

surely going to come this year and the bloody war
would be over! I agreed that this would be a good plan,
so I needed to give him a credible reason for my dis-
embarkation. I told him I had grown up with the love of
my life - that he was a French pilot who had been flying from England, with the free French. My stomach
had always told me when he was on a mission and only
settled when I thought he was safe again. A few days
before they had fished me out of the Rhine, I had been
really quite ill in the stomach. My mother had sat with
me and asked if I were pregnant and instantly, I went
wild at her suggestion, telling her only Albert would
ever be good enough. She knew how intuitive I could
be as her mother had been the same. After a long discussion, and her consulting with her mother, we felt
that Albert must be in trouble. He may be shot down,
injured, or captured, but definitely not dead. With no
communication to the UK or him, we were stumped as
to what to do. My Grand Mother asked if I had a
memento of Mr Albert Noir and of course I said yes. I
went to my room and returned with the one thing I had
of his - a red neckerchief which he had always worn
before he joined the French Air Force. While doing so,
she took a pencil from her bag and tied a thread to it.
Then on some scraps of paper she drew out some fan
shapes. These fan shapers were divided up into quarters. Each quarter, words were written: Injured, Captured, Running, Dead. The next one read France, Germany, Switzerland, Holland. The next one, North,
South, East, West. These fans added up to about seven
or eight in total. She then took them one by one and
held the pencil up by the thread. At the centre bottom of
the drawn fan shape she placed the edge of Albert's
neckerchief under her forefinger. She then seemed to
focus her mind and drift a little. Her right hand was
steady as a rock, even so the pencil started to swing. As
it did so, it would go to and fro over on one part of the
fan shape and one word. Each time she would write the

114

word down that the pencil had been swinging over, then repeat the exercise over the next drawn fan shape. At the end she read out loud to my mother and I the following:

Alive, Injured, Running. North East France / Swiss border. Not Safe!

My mother turned to me and looked me in the eye. She told me that my Gran had the gift, she had never been wrong when she did this. My stomach problem was a similar thing she thought, it was to do with empathy. She surmised that Albert and I were on a very similar frequency, which was why we got on so well. If I were willing to risk my life to find him, she would not stand in my way, but she knew of no way to help me. That night I left home and now I am here I explained.

Cpt Jan Lever whistled lightly at me and looked me up and down across the Bridge as he held the wheel before replying, "My mother had the gift, in two days we will be at a good starting point for you. The river turns and we sail very close to the bank side where, if no rain comes, it will be dry. We will distract the guards and you must jump. We can cover for you and they will forget the fact you have gone over the side in a day or two as they change shifts over and over again. We can do nothing else to help but pray for you."
I was so relieved, "That is enough, I can do the rest!"
He then came back to me very quietly and almost whispered, "I think I know where you learnt to fight as Jo has described it to me. You had me going with your Gran as my mother does do this. If there is anything you want, I don't have it, but I do know a few people in the area you may want to make contact with. Bon Chance little lady."

Two days later we were set. Cpt Laver knew when the

115

guards changed. He somehow organised some clothing that was a little more suitable for the next stage of my journey. He explained the plan they had come up with which was as follows: They would run two lines off the stern over the next few days in the hope they would get a bite or two. The guards would watch and keep an eye on our fishing at first and then lose interest. The two lines would run from either side of the vessel. To keep the lines out of the boats wake and in an area where they may get a bite, they would be held out ten or fifteen feet to the side of the vessel. The only way to do this was to use planks of wood they had on board. They would be secured well enough for a crewman to walk out on and retrieve or lay the lines out as required. Two days further up the river we would come to a bend which was almost 90 degrees as it turned. The Captain would run his vessel tight to the inside bank fractionally too long to ground her near side. To take her away from the shore, he would then spin the wheel hard to port pushing her bow out into the river. The current at first would catch the bow and drive the stern closer to the shore. He now would have to increase revolutions and spin the wheel to starboard to get the ship round the bend. The guards would be enthralled with the excitement while I had my chance to run the starboard plank and jump for it.

The plan worked a treat; I only had to make about fifteen feet in the air from the wood to the long grass and then keep my head down until they were away around the bend and gone. The clothes they had acquired for me weren't great and I had no shoes, but it was enough, thank God! While keeping my head down and staying out of sight until darkness fell, I went over the hand drawn map and information Cpt Laver had been kind enough to give me. As soon as it was reasonably safe to do so I was on the move making my way to my first contact point. As I had been advised, there was the farm

116

that had been described to me. I had been told not to make any form of contact with the occupants but to retrieve what I required from the washing line. Around the side of the farm there would be some pairs of old shoes and boots from the family within. I was to take what fitted best and leave. The occupants were happy to help but wanted no part or involvement that could be traced back to them. This I understood very well and was just sad I could not leave a message to say thank you. Several miles further on I found the next farm I was to borrow from. Here I picked a knife from their tool shed and a few other trinkets including some old field glasses which I knew would come in handy. Well that was it, my lot, with the few Francs my sailor friends had bestowed on me, I was on my way, and in the right direction.

Chapter 11. New Friends.

As I travelled closer to the Swiss border by night and laid up during the day, I wondered how my Uncles' plans were progressing. I knew that through the Bugatti dealership they were given passes to travel over France, delivering spare parts and repairing vehicles. They were definitely the best men to use for getaway drivers, pick-ups and drops on the planet and with access to the best motor vehicles too. I surmised that they used this free-dom to pass and relocate things for the allies and Res-istance at the same time. 'Yep that was them. The Grand Prix Saboteurs.' I chuckled to myself at their bravery, disregard for the authority and their sheer au-dacity. I looked forward to seeing them again when times had changed for the better. I penned them a letter to the dealership with neither named. I knew they would know who it was from. In a form as best I could I advised them that a few things had not gone as as-sumed and a restart was in order. That I would be in contact as soon as it was possible to do so from an ap-propriate location. I then posted it.

While my uncles did their thing I was to seek, recruit and train new personnel. These were to become new Resistance groups. The only advantage was nobody would know them. However the disadvantage was, it was like walking into the lion's den. All the time I would still be looking for Albert.

Eventually and quite by accident, I found two guys who became the mainstay of my team. These were Erich Krahenbuhl - a Swiss man, and Stuart Latimer - an Ir-ishman. I bumped into them when I was looking over a potential target on the Rhine near the Swiss border. I watched them go in, bold as you like, to a river harbour then get onto some barges, move around a bit, and then get off again without bringing attention to themselves.

At the time I thought they must be to do with German security as they moved with such ease around the vessels and security. They then disappeared into the ether as I tried to follow them looking through my field glasses. Just as I was losing them, there were two bloody large explosions in the harbour. The barges they had been on went up in flames with their cargos of fuel. I had to find these guys, this no coincidence; it had to be to do with them. I scoured the roads and hillsides. I could not go into the town; a woman alone with no papers was guaranteed an execution. I knew they had not come from the direction I was in. There was no way they could cross the river for several miles, so they were going to have to go over the next ridge or traverse the side of the mountain in front of me to escape from the valley. I made my way to what would logically be their way out as fast as I possibly could. After an hour or so I reached my next vantage point. Here I sat and waited, then waited some more. Over the past few days I had been able to purloin a small amount of ordinance, which I now hid.

A while later in the baking sun I saw the two leaving the town through my glasses. They appeared to be as carefree and happy as you like. Nobody was asking questions as they sauntered out in my general direction. Well I'd got something right, I hoped. I moved a little to keep a line of sight on them. Ten minutes of walking and laughing, they picked up two horses twenty or so yards inside the tree line. They mounted and started up the trail, close by in my direction. Moving laterally across the hillside, I ventured toward then as they climbed up. Once I knew exactly where their trail would cross me, I prepared for their arrival. In truth there was not much I could do but it kept my mind clear. Positively and with purpose, the horses made their way up the gradient. Just as they approached, I lobbed and pushed a few rocks and boulders. The two

119

horses spooked and both riders stopped chatting and joking. Retiring from the horses was the wise thing to do. It could be that a German patrol was here, or it could be a small land slide. Either way they were better on foot and leading the horses.

I stepped out in front of the two and asked them directly about what I had witnessed. They looked at me calmly, while assessing both their surroundings and me. They could see I was by myself with no back up or gun, so instinctively they tried to jump me. They drew knives and really had a good go. I don't really think they were trying to kill me although later they swore that they were. The fight only lasted a few minutes and once they were both laid out unconscious, I waited for the first to stir. The shorter one stirred first, moaned, and then spoke in English with an Irish accent, "Be Jesus, what the fuook happened?" I sat there and laughed as he started to try and move. He then realised his pants were down around his ankles, his hands were tied above his head onto his friend's hands with one of their sets of braces. The belt from the other one that was used to keep his pants up was now tightened around their necks holding their heads together back to back. He struggled and found it impossible to free himself, as I had also tied their trouser legs together. He then muttered, after he realised his head really hurt, "What the hell are you, a bloody one woman army?" I laughed. I knew I could get on with this Irish fool. He had guts and nerve; he would just need some training and maybe learn to fight a lot better than he had. He was around five foot 8 inches tall when standing, had a tanned unshaven face, his hair was thinning slightly and was bleached by the sun. His sparkling green blue eyes seemed to be full of mischief. I told him that I was known as Murtyl, nothing else, and he told me his name was Stuart Latimer.

At this point the harder one started to stir. I would say he was harder, only because his fighting was much more controlled, he had structure and purpose in his attempted blows. It was only later that I explained how a humble wooden sock-darning dolly had been used to render then both unconscious. Using it like a cloche, a little tap just at the base of the skull behind the ear works a treat. This was the one thing I think the farmer's wife may wonder why I had taken. This other man started the same struggle as Stuart, but soon realised he was not going anywhere until I knew what I wanted to know. So he introduced himself as Erich - a Swiss man from Staffa near Lake Zurich. He was a few years older than Stuart but was smaller in height - maybe five foot four and was a similar build to Kevin Mooney. Obviously, he was also well accomplished with horses, had brown eyes, dark hair, and a weathered look. He was an ex Swiss army chef who wanted to fight. His country was neutral and by the time he was ready, there was only England to join up with, and he stood no chance of getting there to do so. So he came over to Montreux hoping to find a way to do some good, as he put it. He had met Stuart who was working for Charlie Chaplin - gardening, general house duties, and helping in the vineyards, wine presses and generally acted as a gofer. (Going for this and going for that.) Charlie was officially sitting out the war and had been accused of all sorts of shit by the American studios after the WW1. This time, although too old to get involved much, he was doing a few things on the quiet. He was financing these two - officially they worked around the property, but Charlie would help plan some of their clandestine work. He helped them improve basic formulas to make explosives, and then go with them into the mountains to assess its destructive force. Once they had a good formula, the two would drift off on horseback cross country, find the target Charlie had chosen, then find a way to take it out. They would then go back to Charlie's and

121

carry on with life as normal. It tickled Charlie to read in the newspaper, that the Germans could never understand how, with no air or commando raids etc, they could be attacked so far behind the front line.

That had been some information to take in, but if these guys could get in and out of Switzerland without detection, they had to be worth knowing. Risky I know, but my instincts allowed me to go with the flow, I never regretted this. They took me to Montreux, and I stayed with them at Charlie's place. I trained them in combat. They produced explosives, which we moulded into all sorts of shapes - from potatoes to vermin.

Together we carried out several missions while developing a formula. I would write in code to Willy and Robert about a target we thought we could take - such as a railway terminal and yard. When we got the go-ahead via the BBC World Service broadcast, (in code) which would give a date for an air raid in that area, we would be off. The idea was to arrive in the area with a couple of weeks leeway. Erich and Stuart would dig in and hide out with a view of our target. I would get a job in a local bar to fraternise with the locals, while looking for potential Resistance people to assist. I would befriend a high-ranking German Officer if possible. This would be achieved by the following route: borrowing, stealing, or acquiring by some method or other, some rather risqué clothing. This being a well a fitting white blouse, using the buttons only up to a point where privacy of my anatomy was just kept. The collar would be up and my hair down just over my shoulders. I'd wear a black skirt, tight fitting to around my knees, you may call it a pencil skirt with a slit in it. This cut would go up two thirds revealing, when sitting down, a rather larger proportion of my thigh. The lads did think it was a bit raunchy, but it did get those officers excited. My next step took the whole exercise a little deeper. If a

Cheroot were available, I would smoke one - not great but it was fashionable. More interestingly for the Bosch Officer, was to see me drinking. I would order a Champagne Flute glass and quietly ask the barman to fill it with a light local French beer. I'd loudly bet the barman I could drive the Nazi Officer mad just with one drink. As you might guess, they would see the new girl in town, which would be interesting enough, but to see her alone and drinking, while dressed as I did, meant they would not leave me alone (which was of course the idea). They would ask if I were alone, and I would reply that I was and that they could buy me a drink but on a few conditions:

1. They expected nothing in return.
2. They could only buy me the drink I was drinking.
3. They had to guess what it was.
4. They could not touch my glass.
5. They could not smell my glass.
6. They could not ask the barman (who was sworn to secrecy).

They would look at the colour and see the bubbles. They instantly thought it was Champagne with a mixer. As they ran through many ideas they would try and tempt me with Champagnes and other drinks at all sorts of prices. The bar put the prices up as they bought more and more. Once a bottle was opened the fools just drank, never learning what I and the barman had arranged. This made it incredibly easy to pick out a strategic target, and who was the superior, not only by rank but by attitude and natural authority. I would then use the knowledge against them to get what I wanted. It worked a treat on all of our raids in one form or another, as we moved from location to location.

Chapter 12. Reflection.

Nick laid on the big red settee Murtyl had passed away
on. In the lounge they had talked and discussed things
for so long, that she in essence, was still allowing him
to be custodian of. A great shudder ran right through his
body as he read further through the diary. It was now
dawning on him who she must have been, he was
humbled at the fact she had chosen him, to research,
verify and publish her past for the world to know.

Nick had settled down in the past nine years, while
waiting for the first diary to arrive. The lady he had
hoped he would stay with for ever, had become a best
friend and then lover. They had settled together; con-
tentment and peace had settled within their lives and
household as it should. Then things changed, they were
both delighted when Heather fell pregnant - shocked
but delighted. As the pregnancy progressed, all was
well, and their excitement grew as to what the future
held for them as a three. Late in the pregnancy, and too
late to abort, a growth was found in Heather's womb.
There were choices, there always are, but this was a
tough one for both of them. While the foetus was in the
womb, the cancerous growth was in-operable. Chemo-
therapy would be too harsh for the foetus to survive.
Heather was only twenty seven and Nick twenty nine -
very young to go through these kind of choices. The
only person Nick would have like to discuss such a
situation with was Murtyl and she was gone. Heather
had developed (from the stories Nick told her) a deep
respect for Murtyl, what she had done for Nick, in the
knowledge he would do as she asked. It was her turn to
trust Nick as she summoned up all her courage and
hopes for the future.

Eventually a decision had to be made. Nick knew once
Heather had decided what was correct in her mind,

there would be no going back, it was how she had been for as long as he'd known her and one of the reasons he loved her. She had made her decision. She shared her rationale with the man she loved with all her heart. "I love you Nick and am so lucky to have found a most precious friend and the best lover I could ever have hoped for. I have experienced the freedom of loving someone who trusts me implicitly as I trust you. It is the most exquisite, luxurious, emotional, rollercoaster anyone could have dreamt of being on! How can I deny our child the opportunity to grow up with the father I know you will be. As Shakespeare had said: It is better to have loved and lost, than never to have loved at all." Nick knew it would be wrong to attempt to change her mind; it had to be her decision. For all he wanted to, he knew it would be selfish to try and dissuade her. They knew the risks and that was that.

During the birth of their daughter, the growth in Heather's womb ruptured. Everything was done to try and save her, but after ten minutes, she was gone. She never met her daughter but knowing she had been born, she let go of Nick's hand and life, with a smile, tears and, Nick hoped, no regrets. Nick was totally devastated, but now he had Pip, and at three months old, he had his hands full looking after her and keeping the house. He knew he was blessed that he now worked from home and could juggle what he needed to.

Heather had been good with computers and had taught Nick to use the internet and not to just use the computer as a word processor. He was never not going to love Heather and he could already see parts of her in Pip - as he called her, rather than Philippa - the name he and Heather has chosen. He just hoped he could bring her up with Heather's cheek and determination, and then thought maybe a bit of Murtyl's tenacity too; the world would be just a tad surprised with what this produced.

125

Chapter 13. Raids and Results.

My personal aim was to be invited back to the barracks by the highest ranking officer I could.
Allow the chosen ranking officer to drink a little more than the previous few evenings and let him for the first time, get physically close and amorous with me. The arrogance was always the same
and I would play along with it. Usually in a staff car, we would be taken back with a bottle of something, to his place of residence on the installation or camp. These higher ranked officers usually had their own private ballots or accommodation with a batman. I would act a little worse for wear, playing along with the officer's desires. Once the batman had been instructed to retire for the night, it was time to go to work. Men when drunk, are not usually shy in coming forward especially when they are used to having their authority respected. So a little teasing was in order while little more alcohol was supplied to them. Naturally, they would try to become partially undressed, with my assistance, as they fumbled with my attire. It would be around this point I would retire to the bathroom to freshen up and remove a few of my outer garments, while at the same time retrieving a few things from bag. These gents were often married with family photographs around their quarters, or had mistresses which did tend to annoy me, as they had no shame in their intent of having me. However, my intent was one of war, so it did not matter. When they moved in close for the kill in their eyes, the opportunity was there for me to do mine. While in an amorous hold and nibbling each other, I would recover a sharpened crochet needle tucked into the rear and top of my stocking. It was sharpened at the hook end. While gently fondling his scalp with my left hand, my right would wander up his back. Searching for the gap between his fourth and fifth rib. My crochet needle would, with all the enthusiasm I

127

could muster, thrust horizontally and deep into my friend's pericardium. Once punctured, the heart would labour, but with a little tug the hook would catch and tear ventricles, releasing blood pressure and my target could then be laid to the floor. The war was over for them, painlessly.

It was now time to move, and quickly. The first task was to retrieve from my bag a partially burnt cork and black out my face, then dress in the dark slacks and top tightly rolled up in my bag that were on top of my black plimsoles. The clothes I had been wearing were either burnt in the fireplace if the fire was lit or placed by the deceased and doused in the spirits available from the drink cabinet. The one other thing that was always in my bag was a small incendiary time fuse which would be bent to allow the acid within to dissolve the sacrificial wire retaining the spring that would push the striker home and set the device off. They were not accurate on time, but it did give me fifteen to twenty minutes to get to work. From here it was my job to get out of that building to a point on the fence line agreed with Eric and Stuart. Their job had been to set up any help that was on offer that evening. If there were free roaming guard dogs, incapacitate them, allowing me to move in the shadows. Once in the location agreed, they would lob over or pass through the fence more incendiary devices and explosives. The devices I had then were to be dispersed at key point around the installation to cause as much damage as possible when they fired. My next and most important task now was to get off the site, join the lads, and prepare ourselves for the clean-up.

If it were possible and had been accepted by the RAF as a fall back target, we would try to time things to suit their night mission. The idea being our job would be reported as a stray aircraft jettisoning its cargo off target, for whatever reason, resulting the attacking aircraft then aiming for the fire, that we had started. If this were not the case then it was our job to make sure there were no survivors using the weapons we had, so that it could be assumed a roaming allied command force had been in to create the destruction. There were a few around this area and they kept the enemy extremely busy - as we did. I know it should not be the case, but I did enjoy our outings!

On one particular raid, we were late returning from our objective - or the RAF were just a little ahead of schedule. Either way, I caught a blow from the blast from one of the charges they had dropped and was thrown into a boulder, striking my right femur which was now clearly in two parts rather than the preferred one. We were potentially buggered. The lads quickly splinted my leg and we removed ourselves as far away as we could from the target. Once dawn arrived, we needed to reassess the situation and formulate a new exit plan - and agree to separate if required. It was unlikely I could do the three or four days trek over the mountains back to Montreux and the lads could not haul me all the way either, even though they offered. Public transport, trains etc would be under high security and a woman with a broken leg would attract a lot of attention. We sat and pondered our dilemma.

Chapter 14. The Team Was Born.

Eventually Erich came up with a plan that seemed to work for all of us. We were within twenty-five miles or so of Verdun in north-eastern France. He knew of a Monastery there where I may be able to ask for help, or at least be offered sanctuary. We fiddled our way to the outskirts of Dole. Erich bless him, seemed to know his way around the place and got us in - in one go. We skirted various checkpoints and once in the grounds, Stuart stayed with me while Erich approached the big front door and then knocked on it. He was able to obtain a little time with a monk who told him that although he would like to help, they were always being watched by the Germans and continuously checked by them. It was not possible for the monks to become involved in warfare. However once he saw the state I was in, he suggested we wait.

A few hours later, we met for the first time Charles. He appeared out of the dark, asked us to follow him and let us know he was a Monk who came from another part of the Dole Monastery. The Nazis had never found his group of buildings, as its location was hidden by the way the river twisted back on itself as it flowed through the forest by the town. He took us to a crypt to examine me, stating there was no infection, which was a good thing, and he there and then offered to help me. My two workmates would have to trust him and leave me here while they returned to Montreux. It was in Charles's eyes, difficult enough to help a person but to hide and feed three was just too risky. We talked about it and eventually we all agreed that they would return after receiving a note from Charles advising them of my progress. Then they were off, leaving me entrusted to a man we had never met before.

Over the next few days we became friends, conversing

in French even though I was a little grumpy, impatient, and damned right annoying as a patient. It turned out he had travelled all over the east and spent a great deal of time in Tibet and a little in China. He had studied oriental medicine including herbs, acupuncture, and homeopathy as well as many other disciplines. The Abbot had taken to him and used him to treat any sick monks rather than pay the local doctors. So, to a degree as long as he attended prayers, he was given free rein to do as he pleased. He calculated I would be up and moving in under three weeks, which astonished me as in my world a cleanly broken femur was six to eight weeks healing and then you needed to improve your fitness after. So I played along and kept an open mind.

I was placed on a bed where he could bathe me regularly and I could be kept relatively comfortable. My eliminations were to be made possible through a hole in the structure. My first few days there were in light traction; this was achieved by using a weight off the end of the bed structure, connected to a rope which was tied to some straps placed around the injured leg's ankle. Twice a day, he rubbed an oil into my leg that contained arnica, rhus tox and Symphytum, which he said would reduce the bruising and swelling very quickly. It did do this - very quickly! Once the swelling had subsided, he splinted my Femur and braced it so that I could not move it while sleeping. To accelerate the healing process he performed the weirdest thing I had ever seen done. Inserting two acupuncture needles in my upper thigh, one in a spot he named as Biguan (Stomach 31) and the other in a spot he named Liangqui (Stomach 34). He rotated each of the needles together and then individually, in a clockwise motion. After this, he attached a piece of insulted wire by crocodile clip to the end of each needle. He then explained that for a bone to heal naturally, several things must be in place. One: it must start within six weeks of the injury or a new break

131

would have to be initiated by another action for certain things to work within the body. (I did not have to worry about that). Two: the bones should be set, and in our case, we could only use light traction and a splint for support, (in reality he had nothing to set the leg with). Three: the oils had been used and that the acupuncture should do the following:

> The body communicates cell to cell either through chemicals produced by organs and by electricity produced by the mitochondria within each cell. This electricity runs usually at between 3 and 5 ohms. In order for the bone to heal as quickly as possible, he had created an electrical circuit around the break in my femur. The body would naturally complete the circuit allowing one of the broken ends of the femurs to act as an anode and the other a cathode. This would mean that one end of the bone would dissolve slowly, and the other end would receive these calcium ions. This would quickly allow a bridge to develop between the two broken ends of the bone.

He asked me if I could feel anything. I answered that there was a tickle or a trickling feeling where the break was. He smiled, "Well young lady, you can feel it working."
I laughed, "You're joking, how long will it take to be strong?"
His reply was quite startling. "If you agree to allow it to heal properly, and eat as I instruct, and we get plenty of available calcium into you, then you should be walking in ten days and looking to start training lightly with me in fifteen or so!"
I replied, "Surely that's not right? This is a six week plus thing at home!"
"Yes, it is for allopathic medicine and in the modern

medical world, but in my world of Traditional Medicine these things are possible. How many Chinese and Tibetan's do you see walking around with plasters on their legs with crutches?" I had no answer to this as I had never seen a person from that part of the world. Over the next ten days he repeated the exercise with the needles a few times and turned me over to do the same on the Urinary Bladder meridian on the back of the injured leg. Sure enough I was walking fairly comfortably in ten days.

He explained a little about his history and where he had learned this form of medicine and why. He also explained that his skills allowed him to physically take a body from a state of Diss-Ease to a state of Ease, therefore allowing it to heal itself much more rapidly -which is where the other skills came into effect. He then continued to teach me a little of how the Chinese Five Elemental System worked, in an attempt to keep my mind occupied. He also taught me a little about herbs and that essential oils are fantastic tools, but that you have to understand that they are hormones. As such they can directly affect the central nervous system and must be treated with great respect. Every patient should be typed according to the elemental system prior to using them. I found the things he was teaching me intriguing, and in most cases, it seemed to make a great deal of sense. He would also sit and meditate quite close to me. The first time he did this I asked when he finished, or at least seemed to awake again, what he had actually been doing. He replied, "Stepping out, feeling and conveying my electromagnetic energy towards your broken femur to assist in the healing." "No that can't be you making the rough ends of my femur feel itchy and hot can it?" I instantly replied. He smiled, rubbed his hands together while breathing deeply, and placed his open hands, palms toward my body about four inches above me. "I focus my mind and visualise the centre of one palm spinning clockwise and the other spinning anticlockwise. Please let me know what you find." I felt a pushing affect and heat from his right hand and a cool pulling affect from his left. I told him, and he instantly reversed the rotations in his mind. The feeling changed and reversed on my body. He then furthered his explanation, "That is nature's way: sedating was to move in an anticlockwise direction, stimulating was to rotate clockwise." He had decided that if I were willing, he would teach me for as long as I chose to learn. He believed from the few days he had known me that I had an empathy for this. He told me that as I had become stronger, he had been able to feel my presence. I showed no natural aggression but was decisive and willing to take immediate action according to the situation – this was ideal for what he would teach me. He concluded, "Whatever business you are in, this will stand you in good stead by creating a greater balance and sensitivity within you." Then he continued with both the meditation and increasing my awareness of myself and the environment around me. I learnt how to still myself properly, learning and listening more intently than I had ever done or experienced before. It would fit in so well with my S.O.E. I only hoped that this would allow me to become a better agent than my superiors could have hoped!

As my healing progressed, we started to practice martial arts to build my stamina back up, I was surprised at how adept Charles was as an opponent and a training partner.

A few days before the boys returned, Charles told me about a patient he had in his charge. He could not send him back to the UK as he did not have any contacts. The Abbot knew nothing about either his past or the fact that he was helping people such as myself, downed RAF boys, as well as POW escapees. If he were able to help them recover from injury, all he could do then was turn them out, as he had no contact with the outside world, never mind the Resistance. This was a dilemma for him, and he asked if we could help. I explained the mission I was officially on, but not my personal agenda.

He then told me he had a French Pilot in another part of the crypts. He'd had a head injury and Charles was struggling with it all. All physical injuries had healed well, but the bang on the head seemed to have created some emotional problems. Maybe I could meet this man and at least give a view from a different angle, at least as a female if nothing else. I thought why the hell not? I had a few days to go before the lads would be back.

As Charles took me by the hand to lead me to the area this chap was hiding, my stomach started to churn. I then heard the whistle and my knees buckled. As I fell, I turned to Charles and cried out, "You have the man I'm looking for - Albert, don't you?"
Charles was astonished, "How do you know who he is?"
"He is the reason I am here!" I staggered to my feet and ran forward to see Albert. On entry to the darkly lit room I saw him, one hand on a mug of something, whistling, while he sketched something with the other hand. He turned and looked up at me. He obviously recognised me, but that emotion, that sparkle, the glint in his eye was just not there! He stood up and walked over to me, shook my hand, and welcomed me.

As time passed over the next few days, I found the connection was still there but part of him was somehow missing. He trained with Charles and I, thankfully our ability to work as one and move in harmony was still there. Charles watched and was mesmerised by our

135

unity during the exercises in our training sessions. Everything was there except the ability to feel that one emotion. It broke my heart. The lads eventually returned, and between us we explained to both Albert and Charles what we were doing from Montreux. Immediately Albert was in on the action and Charles suggested we use him where we could. As we grew to know Charles better, he became an essential part of the team and this carried on throughout the years.

We started to use Dole as a store, staging post and hide out. We carried out several more missions without mishap, following the protocol originally set up with Uncle Willy and Robert for contact and assistance. At the same time we used the formula that had become so successful.

Chapter 15. The Call Out.

Then it happened. My coded action plan card had gone off to my heroic Grand Prix Uncles and I waited for confirmation from the BBC that our next planned was approved. No approval came. I listened for several nights to the BBC home service at my allocated time. Eventually a coded message was read out, with all the correct markers hidden within. At last we were on again. As I decoded the message I was confused, it was not confirmation of going into action again, but a plea. I had to re-read it several times to understand, believe it and let the information sink in. Essentially it stated, "Chestnut was broken. High ranking members captured by the Gestapo in Paris. Help or neutralise where possible" This was July 14th, 1945.

To me this meant Uncle Willy and Uncle Robert were on the run or captured. They would be tortured for information without mercy and I knew they would not talk. This almost certainly meant death in the most horrific way possible. The request from London was to essentially effect their escape if possible or assassinate my two heroes and anybody else involved. I spoke to the lads and explained the history and what it all meant to me. Without hesitation they all volunteered to help and go to Paris and do whatever needed to be done.

We discussed, planned, and talked, and eventually realised we would have to travel in pairs, as a group of four would arouse far too much suspicion. If we were lucky, we would find help or at least find some local information once we were in Paris. If we weren't so lucky, we would not be alive in a few days' time. We were on the move within 12 hours of the notification. I had no way of communicating with London quickly, so we were absolutely blind and had no contacts, and we had no knowledge of who was safe. We really were on our own. We would be hunted by the Gestapo, the SD the SS and by our friends in the Resistance. Everything we had done before had been supported in some way or another. Not this time, it was possible Robert and Willy were already on a one way ticket to hell, with God know how many others. We had to be on our toes and do what we could, as fast as possible, knowing this could be a one way ticket for us too.

Albert and I took the train to Reims and then onto Paris. We had no in-date forged papers and were going to have dodge the authorities all the way. Erich and Stuart were to travel by road, and the same applied to them. Our aim was to meet three hundred yards west of the west wing of Notre Dame in two days' time at noon. Then if we had made it that far, we were to make our way into the catacombs and try to pick up some local assistance there, if there was any help to be had.

How we made it I'll never really know! At one part of our journey by train, the lady sitting next to me had been holding her child for hours. She was obviously tired and hungry, so I offered to hold her child to give her the chance to sleep for a short while. Shortly after the mother fell asleep, the carriage door opened and in came two men dressed in the Gestapo secret service attire, of trilby and long black leather trench coats. Albert quickly ducked out of the carriage at the other end. He climbed down between the carriages and then hung under ours by strapping himself with his belt to the chassis of the bogey. He somehow hung on until we reached the agreed place for us to disembark. The two men that had entered started to demand identification papers from the carriage occupants. I held the lady's child and as the men approached demanding our papers, I woke her so she could retrieve and produce hers for the Gestapo. I fumbled around in the pockets I could reach while holding the sleeping child. Then I

138

shrugged my shoulders and held my index finger to my lips and motioned 'Shhhhh' and said the baby was sleeping. I quietly asked them to come back in a few minutes so I could find my papers without waking the baby. The two carried on and arrived at the end of the crowded carriage doing their duty, then they turned back, looked me up and down assessing if they could be bothered to return back. I waved a yellowish, old piece of card above my head at them, they made a hand signal that I could only assume meant 'O.K. that will do, we can't be bothered to come and look'. After a short while I passed the child back to its mother. The woman looked at me quizzically then shrugged and minded her own business as people had to do during those terrible times.

Albert and I had agreed to jump a few miles prior to Paris, in the countryside, to avoid the authorities at the station. Those few miles out, he reappeared in the carriage, looking a fair bit grubbier than before he had exited the carriage. We made the jump together, uninjured, and I thought it must be much safer to travel by train than air as both of us had been injured when jumping from our recent flights.

Through good judgment and a lot of luck we safely arrived in Paris. My heart fluttered with pleasure when approaching the wing of Notre Dame Cathedral and I could see my two other partners in crime. They blended in as best they could, to evade being noticed by those devils. Together we headed toward the Arc de Triomphe, to where I had left Albert waiting for us to return. I knew of one entrance to the catacombs, it was cited very low, almost in the gutter at the side of a shop on the infamous Avenue Foch. It was not far from the HQ of those evil Nazis that Robert and Willy had pointed out to me as they had driven passed just those few months before. I had an odd memory of an entrance to

139

the catacombs from when I was young. I knew I had not been into them, but I seemed to remember a big mechanic pointing it out to me all those years earlier, when life was so full of fun.

Once we were in the catacombs we needed to rest, organise food, and watch the dreaded 82 to 86 Avenue Foch. This was to find out what we could, assess the situation and find a way to walk forward with whatever weapons and ordinance we could beg, steal, or borrow. Somehow, we needed to find out which part of the building our targets would be in, and even if they were there or not, then make plans, and then make an attempt. As it happened, a few of the loyal French Resistance were using the catacombs to hide, in an attempt to move around the city un-noticed. One named Christophe - a short chap, with thick spectacles and an ever-smiling face, balding head and as scruffy as they come, settled us in. He had been using the catacombs pretty much as soon as Paris came under German control. He had been part of the Resistance early on during the occupation when it was still individuals fighting in a disorganised manner. Now he showed the active Resistance whenever he could, how to move around the city with the least danger of capture. He had exceptional local knowledge of the catacombs as well as the present situation. He kindly brought us up to speed with who had been captured and where they were being held. It turned out that the German counter-intelligence branch of the SS - known as SicherheittsDienste or the SD, also used Numbers 82, 84 and 86 of Ave Foch. He advised us, and I just seemed to trust him. Number 84 was used specifically for the imprisonment and torture of captured suspected S.O.E. agents in France. There were frequent transfers of these prisoners from No 84 to Fresnes Prison on the outskirts of Paris. The second floor housed the SD's wireless section controlled by Joseph Goetz, from where the radio games with the

S.O.E. were conducted using captured wireless sets and codes from captured codebooks. I was shocked to learn this, I was so pleased that the transmitter and code books I had brought with me had been destroyed, they could have resulted in me being in the rooms over the road at the wrong end of the questions. The fourth floor, we were instructed, was taken up as the offices and private quarters of Stormbannfuhrer Josef Kieffr, who was in absolute control of that part of the building and the things that went on inside of No 84. On the fifth (top) floor were the guards' rooms, and interpreters' offices, as well as the cells used for the confinement of prisoners undergoing interrogation. It was at this point Christophe was able to tell us that Uncle Willy had actually been captured earlier and it would seem he had held out through all his interrogators actions, then he had been taken to Berlin for further questioning by even more intense beings directly under Hitler. It had been rumoured that Hitler had actually met Willy personally. It just showed how little I knew. He was unable to tell me too much about Uncle Willy's capture but was able to confirm he had not divulged any information as there had been no repercussions or an increase in activity by the Boch, or an increase in captured agents. Christophe was very sorry that nothing had been done to help Willy be freed; he just hoped Willy Grosvenor Williams - the brave hearted racing driver was still alive.

Chapter 16. Listening

We came to a point of rest within the catacombs where all five of us could stretch out with the dim light available from two candles. The four of us relaxed as best we could as Christophe started to divulge information. This was a lot more than just disturbing regarding my Uncles. The actual situation in Paris as it was now compare to what it was when I was a little girl and those great days with such wonderful people was more than just a little disturbing.

On the day of Willy's capture, at around 0930 hours, a number of German vehicles had arrived at Willy's home near Auffargis. He had been spending more and more time at his home with his wife, whilst doing some crazy stunts with Robert in fast cars preparing for the allies to land in the near future. There were around 15 German officers in plain clothes, under the command of Karl Langer. He was a typical SS Officer, in his long black leather coat strutting around shouting orders to his own men and demands towards the house, with an electric loudspeaker. They went straight for Willy - Langer was not subtle, his starting gambit was to have the front of the house strafed with 50 calibre rounds until very little of the front of the house was left. Inevitably, Willy had to show himself and be captured. His only request was that they leave the house in a repairable state and his wife alive. This was done, but the rest of the estate was searched in a manner that it had never been searched before. They actually had little evidence against Willy Grover Williams, but Langer was on a mission. Only a few days earlier in the dead of night, while radio detection vans were homing into a suspected spy, a silver fish-tailed missile of a car had flown past one, then two of his units. Nobody could describe just how fast this car was going, other than like a rocket and it had two occupants. Langer had done his homework well. He knew that anyone could drive fast, but not too many would survive to do it again. Anybody could build a fast car, but this one went round corners he had been told. Thirdly, it must use fuel - and a lot of it. The question was, who could drive like this? Who could hide a car like this and who could get hold of the fuel to use it? That calculation had allowed him the authority to put his raid team together. The property had been searched to no avail in the past, now his team was going to do the job properly. Win or lose, he believed in his calculations.

The first seal for Willy's future was found down a well. A false bottom a few feet below the water level was seen from the top. They broke through it and found several unopened RAF supply canisters full of weapons. Langer tutted at Willy while shaking his head. The searched carried on. In the stables they kicked and banged around and eventually found a wall freshly pointed up behind some straw. Six men produced a battering ram and broke through it. Behind that wall were fifty two more incriminating canisters containing enough weapons and ammunition to supply a small army. They still had not finished the search. Eventually, hidden in the woods and camouflaged over, they found the bare metal aluminium prototype Bugatti - the rocket that had been witnessed. He was taken away and not allowed to speak with anyone. During the search period, Langer ordered a Spaniard called Mr. Jean to soften the prisoner up. The SD often used foreigners to do their dirty work against suspected SOE agents. Mr Jean enjoyed his work and was a complete bastard, as well as a traitor.

While this was happening, Maurice Benoist (the brother of Robert) arrived at Willy's home 'Auffargis' with Vogt and a guy called Peters who was working for the SD. Peters real name Pierre Cartaud. He knew all about the British backed French Resistance, simply because until his arrest in May 1942 he had been a part of it. Code named 'Capri', he had acted as a courier for Colonel Remy's intelligence in Bordeaux, supplying information to the British about German movements. After his arrest he worked for the Nazis, and information he gave them led to the arrest of hundreds of individuals within Remy's network. From there, Peters put all his energy into catching British agents, his motive

143

*was not anger toward the allies but easy money from
the Nazis. After only a year, the Nazis had absolute
confidence in his ability to rat out allied agents. In return he had the authority to roam anywhere he chose.*

*Maurice and Willy were taken back to the fifth floor of
Avenue Foch by Vogt and Peters. Maurice was released
quite quickly, which led Willy to be suspicious of his
allegiances.*
*Willy, during his stay there, was able to pass a message
to his wife Yvonne, via a cleaner who recognised him
for the hero he was. It read: 'There is little hope, you
must leave Paris straight away.' She reacted instantly
and hid for the next three weeks at a friend's house in
Thoren, just north of Grasse, before heading out toward
the coast.*

*At 1930 hrs that evening Willy's interrogation was star-
ted by Vogt. It lasted all night - unrelenting heavy duty
questioning, water boarding, being knocked about by
big bruising fists on the end of heavy outer hitters who
gain pleasure from their employment. It was not believed that Willy had talked but they seemed to know all
about the Chestnut cell. It is thought they hoped they
had one of Chestnut's leaders, but that has not been
confirmed to my knowledge. However, they were after
Robert Benoist as they knew the two spent a lot of time
together. Steadily they were closing the net and intensi-
fying the search to heights never witnessed in Paris
before.*

*Vogt knew he had a high ranking S.O.E. man in front of
him, or at least he must be high up in the Resistance
after finding such an arsenal of arms. Robert had gone
to ground as Paris was becoming too hot for him to
move, never mind operate in any longer. He stayed low
for a day or so but soon felt he needed to know what
was going on in the city, and not least with his mother*

144

and father. He did not attempt to contact any of his Resistance personnel, as he knew they were probably being watched, captured or in hiding themselves. He sought out a post office that was out of the way and did not seem to be under surveillance. He took his time and then decided to risk using the telephone in the kiosk there. Knowing all calls went through switchboards, it would take a few moments to be put through to the receiver of his call. All he needed was to hear one of his parent's voices, to know they had not been taken prisoner, and then he could hang up and go back into hiding. He made his call and waited. It was taking a lot longer than usual. After forty or so seconds he decided to hang up before being connected. He left the Post Office, but it slowly dawned on him that the operator at the exchange had a strong German accent and his parents' telephone number would probably be on a watch list and under surveillance. The Post Office was in the Place Gambetta. He did not know the operator had already reported to the SD at Avenue Foch, that an unknown man was attempting to call Benoit's parents from there. The Germans reacted positively and quickly, having teams on the move within seconds to try and apprehend this suspect. Robert walked briskly away down the street. A gent approached from behind him, dressed in civilian clothing and spoke out loud, "Bonjour, Monsieur Benoist." Robert noted the man had spoken in French, but his guttural accent just sounded all wrong to be a real Frenchmen, so he ignored it. The unknown man repeated himself; he was in such close proximity that Robert just could not ignore him again. He turned and looked blankly at the person, hoping to bluff his way out of danger by saying it must be a case of mistaken identity. The man continued to speak to Robert - he was stalling. Robert realised this as he noticed several men approaching from different directions towards the two of them. A car pulled up, Robert knew it was too late to run as the men took hold of him and roughly bundled him into the back seat. There was no escape, all he could do was relax as best he could and hope for an opportunity. Three men were left behind in the street. Robert had one of the thugs sitting either side of him in the rear of the car. The other two were in the front with one driving and one pointing the muzzle of a Luger at his chest. He protested his innocence, but his captors ignored his pleas and drove on towards Avenue Foch in all haste to their superiors. The rear of the car was relatively narrow and shoulder room was tight. Robert raised his arms over and around the shoulders of his captors to reach and hold the hand loops hanging down from the upper rear door posts to steady himself as the car raced through the streets of Paris. As the car was cornered, it rolled heavily on its overloaded soft suspension. In this particular model the leather strap that Robert was holding acted (when pulled at an angle) as the door opening devices. He waited, hoping that this was going to give him that one chance he needed. The logical route his captors seemed to be following Robert knew would take them past the large department store behind the opera house, then they would continue up Boulevard Haussmann until they reached the Arc de Triomphe. From there it would be just a few hundred meters to their destination. He worried there would be no opportunity to make a break on this route. But the driver then took an unexpected turn at the junction of rue de Richelieu, probably heading for the Ministry of Interior where the Gestapo also had offices. Taking the opportunity as the car swung right, he lurched himself at the German next to him and at the same time released the door. The German rolled out of the car with Robert close behind; he used the German to break his fall on the cobbled street. In an instant he was on his feet and running. The car had skidded to a halt, there was confusion behind. He ran ducking and diving between pedestrians, by the time the Germans were aware Robert was not lying in the road

146

with their colleague, he was gone.

Robert ran into the arcade Passage de Princess and cut through from rue de Richelieu to the Boulevard de Italians. Here people surrounded him as he quietly made his way through to Boulevard Haussmann and assessed the damage to his clothes. He knew he looked out of place with the tears in his clothing, so he needed to change. He headed down Avenue Foch to try and find his old friend from WW1 - Pilot and racer, Roger Labric, who had an apartment next to Salle Pleyel concert hall. From there at least he could make a call to a faithful employee at the Bugatti garage and speak to someone he trusted to find him some new clothes, and then make his way to a car he had hidden.
His employee L'Antoine answered his call from his friend's home. Robert spoke first.
"This is Robert," he stated before L'Antoine could speak. "Meet me at 16 Avenue Foch." There was a pause.
"You mean at Bugatti's?" L'Antoine asked.
"Yes." Robert replied and rang off. He was worried that if he stayed on the line too long the call would be traced or at least listened to. What Robert didn't know was that when L'Antoine had answered the telephone, he was surrounded by four Germans menacing him with guns. Two were in uniform carrying machine guns and two in plain clothes. They had only burst into L'Antoine's moments before, demanding to know where Robert Benoist was. They threatened to take him and his wife to prison if he did not cooperate. He had no idea what had happened to him or where Robert was. Then the telephone had rang just after they had arrived! The two plain clothes Germans had heard everything. They demanded L'Antoine drive them immediately in Benoist's car to Avenue Foch. His wife would be held captive by the uniformed soldiers to guarantee his compliance. What only L'Antoine under-

*stood was in Robert's rush he had made a supposed
mistake when he had stated that the Bugatti offices
were at 16 Avenue Foch. In fact there was nobody in
the building called Bugatti. Ettore Bugatti's apartment
and drawing office were several hundred meters further
up Avenue Foch. L'Antoine dropped the two Germans
off at No 16 – as instructed, and they disappeared off to
find the Bugatti apartment. They were confused by the
ensuing answers they received, which surmounted to
nobody called Bugatti lived in the building. The Germans were not quite sure what to do, but they had
heard the conversation, so they decided to wait in the
car outside expecting Robert to emerge from hiding at
some point.*

*Robert was unable to see what was going on below
from Labric's apartment. He decided to call the Bugatti
office and talk to Ettore's secretary George Clavel - a
man he knew he could trust. He asked Clavel to see if
his car was waiting outside. Clavel went outside to
look, then returned to tell Robert it was standing several hundred meters further down the road. L'Antoine
was in it, but there was also two other men sitting in the
back seats. Clavel thought it may be a trap and advised
Robert to find another way out of the building he was
in. Labric's apartment was on the top floor with access
to the roof. Robert decided to sit it out on the roof. With
Labric in the apartment, if it was searched there should
be no reason to go up there. As he climbed up, the air
raid sirens began to sound. Everybody headed for the
air raid shelters but Robert knew he could not risk being caught in one. Labric latched the skylight and left
Robert on the roof.*

*Once it was dark and Labric had not returned, Robert
made his way across the rooves to Salle Pleyel next
door. He broke in through a skylight and left a message
to say he would pay for the damage he had caused. He*

148

*then made his way to the ground floor where he was
challenged by the night watchmen. They had a little
banter and a drink then Robert asked if the night
watchmen would check there were no Germans on the
street. The watchmen returned and gave Robert the all
clear to go. Knowing the midnight curfew was coming
soon, he did not risk trying to traverse the city. He
could not go to any of his known friends, and so made
his way to a family he had met once or twice. He asked
Monsieur Dupuy if they could put him up for the night,
as he had been caught out by the curfew. They agreed,
having no knowledge of Robert's activities. He left before the family awakened in the morning, so trying not
to place them in danger.*

*The Germans asked Charles Escoffier - the owner of
Grand Garage de la Place Clichy in the rue Forest if
the car he stored in his garage was Robert Benoist's. It
was and they took it. So when Robert telephoned from
the local Café, he was told the Germans had taken it.
Robert then waited for office hours and telephoned the
Bugatti showroom on the Avenue Montaigne to speak to
his secretary - Stella Tayssadre. She knew from Clavel
that Robert was on the run from the Germans and she
took no persuading in offering to help him. They arranged to meet, she took him to her family's apartment:
67 Boulevard Ponaitowski, in the South East of Paris.
She then returned to work promising she would come
back with updates on what was happening. The next
day – a Saturday, Robert decided to try again to make
contact with Henri Dericourt by going to their usual
rendezvous at the Ping Pong Bar on rue Brunel, just off
the Avenue de la Grande Armee. He told the SOE Air
Movement Officer what had happened and that he must
leave France as soon as possible. Henri agreed and
assured Robert that he would find space for him on one
of his secret flights to the U.K. Henri promised he
would telephone Stella at the Bugatti garage when all*

was arranged, using the pass phrase, "Do you have news of Maurice?"

For twelve days Stella was Robert's eyes and ears. She passed everything on she heard in the Bugatti offices and made contact with several survivors of the networks for him. Robert was informed there could be no flight out until later in August because the moon would be too bright. He was going to have to sit it out, there were too many paper checks on the streets, so he had to sit tight in the apartment. Robert Benoist was actually only second on Henri Dericourt's list of priorities. Nick Boddington had been flown in from England, to independently assess the damage to the networks. The Germans knew he was there and were intent on finding him. Henri had to insist on Nick hiding outside of Paris in the country. When the moon was favourable, Henri had flown Nick out by a two seater, single engined Lysander - from near Tours. He then allowed his priorities to roll round to others in trouble. He actually had eight agents who desperately needed to leave France and return back to England. This was way too many for a Lysander to do. In the end they used a Lockheed Hudson - once Henri had located a suitable landing area.

The flight Robert was on recovered SOE agents from all over France. It was a very daring pick up, or stupid, looking at the list of SOE operatives' names listed on the flight. Once landed in England, they were all taken to the Royal Victoria Patriotic School in the middle of Wandsworth Common. It was not a very welcoming building and Robert felt like it was a prison. It gave the British time to go through everybody's stories. Once they had picked through all the information given, it was found that one of the returned SOE agents was a double agent acting for the Nazis. Although they still scrutinised all of Robert's encounters and escapes from the Germans, there was really never any doubt of alle-

giance to the allies. He was soon allowed to roam freely while staying in one of the SOE's safe houses in the West End. It was a long time since he had been in the U.K. when racing at Brooklands. All he could think of was returning to France as soon as possible. He wanted to know what had happened to his parents, his wife, and his friends. What had happened to Willy Grover? All the time he could not bear the thought of Paris still being occupied by the Nazis.

His debriefing started two weeks after his return, the SOE decided he was exactly the right sort of chap to be in France helping with their work. They would train him properly over a few months while the search for him in France settled down. He would then be sent back to continue Willy Grover's work. So he began a three-week course in explosives at 17 Brickendonberry, under George Rheam's instruction. He was sent on many refresher courses and was given a commission as a Second Lieutenant on the General List of the British Army. From there on after, he only appeared as a British Officer on the secret War Office lists. He was sent back to France to work around the port of Nantes on the mouth of the river Loire. His codename was Lionel, and he was given the alias of Roger Bremontier. This meant that all his initialled belongings could still be used. He was to pick up on Willy's work whose organisation was now to be called Clergyman. Clergyman was to consist of four completely separate cells, each with its own targets. One cell was to be used as a reception committee for arms and explosives. Another was to target railway lines and links. The third one was to go for electrical pylons lines and to put them out of action for at least a week on D Day. The final one's aim was to devise ways of stopping the Germans from destroying the Port of Nantes.

He was given half a million Francs and told to contact

151

nobody from the old network around that area. His mission was to last around two months; he would be arriving in France during the January moon without the assistance of a wireless operator. He was to contact a well proven wireless man called Hercule, operating from and around Le Mans. Hercule had been a professional radio operator in the 1930's but in 1940, when he was given an English radio set to use, he found it difficult. So he had been transported to England and trained by the SOE. While away, his wife and daughter had been arrested by the SD. He was regarded so highly by the SOE, he was given free rein to work for any SOE organisation, and as many as he liked. He worked for at least six different networks and sent 138 operational messages. His secret was to never stay in one place more than one night so he was always on the move, resulting in the Germans struggling to keep up with him.

Robert was near to Paris. In order to find out what had happened to his network, he caught up with L'Antoine - his old mechanic, who checked that his Citroen truck was still available. During this time, it came to light that Robert's brother Maurice had got into bed with the Germans and was passing information on. This was confirmed when Maurice was witnessed at the arrest of two other agents. Robert wrote anonymously to as many people he could, to advise them not to trust his brother. L'Antoine and Robert then set off for Nantes with all the equipment they could recover from old hiding places that had been missed by the Nazis.

On route RN10 they tried to avoid check points by taking as many back roads as possible. Eventually they were stopped by a German military policeman and advised they had too many gas cylinders in the vehicle. They were then told they must take the policemen into the city and have the vehicle checked over. They knew

152

this was bad news. Robert offered to sit in the back of the truck, as it had only two seats in the front. While travelling, Robert lifted as much equipment as possible and jumped with it. He then made his way back to Paris. During this trip, his suitcase with all his clothes and ID papers sewn into the lining were destroyed.

The SD were handed what was left and so now had Robert's new ID as well as knowing he was back in Paris. They quickly brought his brother Maurice in to identify what was left of Robert clothing to confirm this. In the meantime, L'Antoine had arrived at the Police HQ on Places de Epars in Chantres and was told to unload the truck. He knew this meant arrest and claimed Robert had been a hitch hiker, and that he did not know him. As he unloaded, he waited until the guards were caught up in their own conversation, then made a run for it through the narrow streets. The guards chased, firing shots off where they could. Eventually, with no energy left, L'Antoine dived into a Florist, they hid him immediately and he just escaped capture. Later he realised how lucky he had been as he found a bullet hole through the bottom of his trouser leg.

Robert stole a bicycle and rode twenty or so kilometres away from Paris and reassessed the situation. When he had lost his clothing, he had also lost the Wireless transmitter, frequency crystals and all the false German blank passes. He decided to rent a flat in Paris and used the psuedonym Daniel Perdrige. The real Daniel Perdrige was a member of the communist party and had been arrested in 1941 for inciting Resistance. He was one of the 99 hostages executed at the Fort du Mont-Valerian in Surenes December 1941. This was a reprisal for the killing of one German officer. Sadly, Daniel had left two little girls. Daniel had a sister who had worked with Robert as part of Chestnut operation,

153

*her code-name was Sonia. He stayed with her for a
short time as he realised he had no way of contacting
Hercule because the bar he needed to go to make contact with him had just had its owner arrested. However,
the Ping Pong bar's owner - Henri Dericourt was in the
South of France for another few months. He had no
way of communicating with him, so he decided to make
his way to Nantes under his own steam.*

*Nantes was a difficult town to navigate and be safe in
because of its strategic value as a port, it had the first
bridge over the Loire. The Allies carried out two
massive bombing raids within a week of each other, the
first killed 1400 people and destroyed 700 buildings
and caused much more damage. The second raid destroyed 800 buildings and 200 people were killed, the
fire following from the raid burned for three days.*

*Robert now returned to Paris, and on December 1,
1945 he met Yvonne Grover Williams with Mme Fremont at the Brasserie Sherry on Point des Champs
Elysees. They had arranged to meet with Stella, to discussed Maurice (Robert's brother) as a traitor. They
also discussed Willy as he was now being held back in
Fresnes - a Swiss delegation had gained the release of
one man who had been held there for four months. He
had told Mme Fremont that Willy had never talked but
Maurice wandered around secure areas never being
stopped.*

*Robert returned to Nantes and started to set up new
networks. He soon realised that even with men, without
the explosives they required, they could not do their
job. He recruited an ex Algerian boxer called Pet-
rouche and started to work from a different angle: assassinate proven collaborators; gather information
about the SD; and make the Germans aware that they
were coming for them. They targeted Karl Boemelberg,*

154

*the head of the Gestapo in France, who was now oper-
ating from Avenue Foch. The SD Chief (Joseph Kieffer)
who they knew had interrogated Willy, lived at Avenue
Foch just below the prison cells on the fourth floor.
They also listed Hanri Lafont, a known criminal whose
gang worked for the SS from a house on rue Lauriston,
they attacked at any opportunity they had.*

*Robert returned to England and demanded silenced
pistols, machine guns, incendiaries devices, grenades,
and knives - he was an angry impatient man, to say the
least. This was granted and, on his return, Partouche
proved to be an even more exceptional ally. Masquer-
ading as a sympathiser, he was able to discover where
and when the Germans were going to do their unan-
nounced spec raids. These raids would round up 40 to
50 people and check their papers. It was done in a hope
that they may flush out collaborators and SOE agents.
For Robert and Partouche this was ideal, Robert would
pass the information on to his men and attack in force
the Nazi inquisitors.*

*Once again Robert returned to England. He was al-
lowed to return to France as D Day approached and
was sent to Nantes with the same objectives as before:
recruit, train, arm and destroy when requested. He was
given several code phrases to memorise that would be
broadcast by the BBC warning him when D Day was
imminent and what to attack with all the Resistance
men he was able to muster. Once this was organised, he
would be free to go back to Paris to continue his activities there. He was given his own wireless operator -
Denise Bloch who was a Jewish athletic girl. She had
evaded capture several times and been a wireless operator since 1942. She had done well and was one of the
few to survive in the business she was in. This time
Robert made sure his brother did not know he was back
in Paris.*

155

It was around about this time that Robert decided to approach Jean Pierre Wimille. Willy Grover had not allowed this earlier, but times had now changed. Even though Wimille was 13 years Robert's junior, they had been race partners and really great teammates driving for Bugatti. They won at Pau and at the Le Mans 24 hr before Wimille had the bad road accident. He came back later that season and on a skiing trip, met his future wife Cric. She was a beautiful, slender lady with dark hair, who fought alongside Jean-Pierre for the Resistance, she only just escaped from, being sent to a concentration camp in Germany, in August 1944. Jean-Pierre was a qualified pilot and had been conscripted to fighter training school at Etampes. After the German invasion, he was demobilised and married Cric. He tried to convince the Vichy government to support a racing trip to an Indian Appolis meeting in the USA. This was denied so they sold their estate and moved closer to Paris. Wimille, with the help of an ex Bugatti engineer, started to design cars for post war production.

Robert recruited Wimille into his network under the code name of Giles. On the evening of June 5 1945, Robert Benoist heard the messages from the BBC he had for so long been desperate to hear. He then immediately put his teams into action around Nantes. The following evening, out of 1050 raids planned and acquired arms for, 950 were completed by his teams of saboteurs. His groups halted the movement of all German troops and vehicles in the area of the Dourdon-Rambouillet for quite a while. Robert Benoist, with as many men as he could muster, returned to Paris where the Germans were making as many arrests of suspects as they could. Robert's group created as much confusion as was humanly possible to keep the Nazis off balance.

156

Robert's mother had become very frail during her four months detained in Fresnes prison. She died at the age of 68 soon after her release. Robert did try to go and see her but was unable to in time. He witnessed the funeral from a distance, while remaining hidden at a safe distance. He needed to stay in a safe house that was close, as the curfew made it too dangerous to traverse the city at night. On his return to the safe house, there were four SS officer waiting for him. He was unarmed and helpless. His captors called Avenue Foch to let them know they had Benoist and waited for instructions.

Early in the morning, Benoist was taken to the SD HQ - straight to the fifth floor for questioning. He did not give any information away, even though methods of questioning had relaxed since the time of Willy Grover's ordeal; it was still very nasty indeed. Over a period of a few days, 80% of Benoist's SOE agents were captured. Some of these were able to talk their way out of custody and some were not. Now Wimille stepped up and tried to put the operation back together. Sadly he failed, but only to a degree.

It was August 24, and the Allies were well on their way to Paris, Vogt invited Benoist's brother to visit Avenue Foch and bring Robert a change of clothes. Benoist asked his brother to pay his rent on the flat and used the opportunity to tell the maid Chiquita who was with, that he believed he had been given away by an English woman Violette Szabo. However, this was never confirmed. Maurice informed his brother that he was being deported to Germany the next day!

I cried as Christophe delivered all this overwhelming information. We had obviously missed the chance of helping at Avenue Foch. I let him carry on as there was

157

obviously more to say. As he told us what was going on and brought us up to date, I noticed he was in terrible shape. He pulled away from any candlelight that was offered up to him even in the darkness of the Catacombs. As my eyes had grown more accustomed to the dim light I began to see why. His skin was white and waxy. A slightly putrid odour seemed to follow him, and he shook all the time as if he were cold. He looked damp, if that was possible. Then I noticed he had no eyelids; he could not blink even if he tried. He hid his eyes from the light by bobbing his head forward and allowing his flat cap to protect them, until they became accustomed to the light in front of him, it was awful to watch. He had no hair on his face or head that I could see - just burns and scars. These were nothing like what I had seen before. Glancing down I could make out he had no fingernails, as he scrabbled his fingers on the floor to retrieve a piece of paper he had dropped. Even though there was room to stand in the cavernous part of the catacombs we were in, he did not do so. His ankles were twisted where he had been hobbled. He had not been born like this; it had been done to him. As Christophe moved, there was a rolling motion to his crawling. Wherever we got to, there would be a bench set up that he could rest at with a low table he could lean on. I could not imagine what he must have been through. A few tears started to roll down my face, he held out a hand. Using the back of his forefinger he gently and lovingly lifted the tear from my cheek and smiled at me revealing a black hole with no teeth. I shut my eyes and asked, "Who and When?"

"I worked with Willy Grover, I was one of his mechanics, do you not remember me, we have met many times before. When you were a little girl you came around the garage on my shoulders as we followed Willy and Robert round the workshop looking to improve the cars. We discussed ideas for modifications and improvements. When they taught you to drive, I was always there with the starting handle to spin your Austin's engine over after you stalled it. If it broke, I fixed it for you. Can you not remember 'Christophe le Grand'?" At this moment I remembered who he was, and my emotions began to well up inside me. He carried on talking "The Boch never knew Mr Grover and I had a friendly connection outside of the garage. Their class system meant this could not be. They knew I was with the Resistance but had no idea how close he and I had worked together. The day Willy was taken away to Berlin, I was dropped off at hospital, to recover again from my treatment from the kind and well-meaning Miss Ranndue. It was from the hospital I was brought here by a few very special and brave nurses - Anna and Rachael, with doctors Thomas and John, in effect they secretly evacuated me from the hospital. I never saw those caring people again, but for a while medication seemed to appear allowing me to sleep. Maybe they were caught or moved I have no idea. Since then the Catacombs have become my home. I help the Resistance where I can and gather data for the Allies when they arrive. When this is all over, I hope to organise a new form of Resistance, the type all will cheer for, even though they will know nothing of who we are. The Authorities will have to turn a blind eye to our activities. To repair the things that are broken in this the great City of Paris. We will repair the clocks in the towers that do not work. We will take away the broken things high up that people never see and return them in perfect order. My volunteer army of artisan's will be unknown and unseen like myself! Sorry I digress sweetheart. Miss Ranndue works for Vogt, she is particularly vicious and where he found that 1.35m piece of hell I will never know." He spat on the ground as his eyes watered and glazed over. He paused for a second and then carried on, "When you think it is over and you want to give up and die, she sits and waits like a Praying Mantis. You dare not move or show signs of life as she

watches from somewhere. Arriving in her pristine
laundered civilian clothes, she smiles at you. Her little
pointy ears, pixy eyebrows disguise the hell she has
been dreaming up for you that day. Petite and slim,
those blue eyes and mousy coloured hair give nothing
away of the anger and pain that must be inside her. I
think she never treats the woman prisoners with her
particular kind of love. Little games such as matches
under your fingernails being lit, are such soft lovers
things to do."

"Oh my God!' I exclaimed.

"She will drill through a man's fingernails one at a time
with the wrists tied down, so the hand and fingers are
immobilised. This is done one at a time, maybe two
fingers or toes a day. With clay, a little funnel would
then be placed and moulded into a funnel over the drill
hole. Just as you would to put acid into a lock, or when
playing with plastics shaping explosives. Then slowly
an acid would be placed into the clay funnel. This
would start to tickle for maybe two or three seconds. I
think it must have been Sulphuric acid as it was quite
thick and seemed to hunt water. Once it was through
the unbroken skin under the drilled nail it went wild.
The pain was so intense I fainted several times, only to
wake up in a cell with a clean, throbbing undressed
wound. These were so tender, a breath of air sent me
into agonising pain. You remember my height and my
hair? My scalp was burnt with an acetylene torch and
my ankles broken so many times I cannot remember. A
bag over the head, your head held back, and water
thrown over it continuously so you cannot breathe is
child's play to her. I know she worked at a concentration camp and loved to tap away at Jewish captives'
privates with a pencil. Gently tapping away for such a
long time, that over a day or two the testis turned black.
This was just repeated every day for no reason other
than her pleasure of hurting men. God, what is in her
mind? I do not know. Since the Allies landed, she has

160

travelled north - I think to Holland. It could be Amsterdam, Rotterdam, or Utrecht. She could be anywhere with another sneaky sick bastard! I am sure this will be to hide, and come the end of the war, play the innocent. If you see her, do not be taken in by the smile and the gestures. Be warned, you will be dispatched without a thought entering her head, just as a mouse in a trap - thoughtless, deadly and with intent. I pray she does not team up with others with such malice within themselves." I grimaced, as did Albert, Erich, and Stuart as the realisation of the terror in Christophe's eye unveiled the rest of the truth. My stomach had churned to see this gentle man, who had been mutilated into such a physical mess. He obviously still had the heart of a lion as he had mentioned how he planned for the future. There was nothing we could do to help him, but maybe we could still help Uncle Willy and Uncle Robert. If anyone had an idea of what was going on and where, Christophe did.

Chapter 17. The Chase

As the Allied troops were battling their way out of
Normandy, the number of executions was sadly increasing day by day. We were told that Robert had been
sent to Fresnes where nearly 3000 prisoners were being
held. This was nearly half the total number of prisoners
being held in the whole of Paris. The prison was badly
overcrowded, and the prisoners were very jumpy. Each
morning, the prisoners waited to find out who would be
facing a firing squad. They found out by listening to the
iron wheeled carts as they delivered coffee (acorn) to
the inmates in cells along the corridors. If the cart
passed a cell, the prisoners within knew they were staying. If the cart stopped at a cell, the prisoners would
then be informed who was to be executed, and who was
to be deported.

It was August 8th, and Uncle Robert was now being
deported with a very special group of prisoners. I urged
Christophe to hurry as it was now August 9th, we had
no time to plan, but maybe we could still do something.
The prisoners who were suspected or known spies had
been assembled onto three prison buses. The first two
were for males and the last one for females. They were
nearly all SOE agents from all around France. I do not
know how many Robert actually knew. They all quietly
glanced and acknowledged each other but nobody
spoke, nobody knew who maybe an infiltrator and who
were using what aliases. It would be safer to acknow-
ledge a friend at a better time. Before they boarded the
buses, the prisoners were hand cuffed into pairs and
handed an International Red Cross food parcel. This I
can only assume gave a little hope and encouragement
or it was just for show and they were empty. The buses
departed and quickly drove through Paris to Gare de
L'Est, where the Germans were putting a train together
to run across north-eastern France to Germany.

162

By the time we arrived, the train had already left, and we raced to find a way to follow. Christophe took us out of Paris by routes none of us would ever have found or could remember. Sadly, I never saw him again. I hope he survived; he did more for us in a few hours than I can ever remember or could have thanked him for.

Once we were out of Paris, we were able to pick up the railway line that Christophe had suggested would be the most likely route. He had drawn a map that was pretty accurate. He had also suggested a few farmers that may be able to help us with horses, as well as Velo's (a small two stroke pedalled motor bike) that we could borrow to travel quickly on less well check-pointed roads. With his map he also supplied us with a time piece and compass. He drew on the whereabouts of checkpoints and fuel depots for vehicles. It took us a day to get ahead of the train using every bit of guile and speed we could muster. The train was a converted troop carrier which was also returning injured soldiers from the retreating front. By this time, the Allies had almost complete control of the air and so the Germans painted Red Crosses on the carriages. The American P47 Thunderbolt fighter-bomber pilots were aware of this and would attack anyway. The last carriage on this train had an Anti-Aircraft gun on it, as many had been attacked and some destroyed. The prisoner carriage was coupled to the Anti-Aircraft bogie. It housed several guards as well as the prisoners, we were later to find out that the prisoners were housed as follows: nine handcuffed pairs into one compartment, eight handcuffed pairs into another and three female prisoner into another part with the guards. There was no ventilation and all the windows had been knocked out and then boarded over. In the carriage were probably the SD's most wanted men and woman, including Stephaney

Hessel - one of General de Gaulle's secret agents, Yeo Thomas, Major Henri Frager, Squadron Leader Maurice Southgate - a legend in the South West of France. About half of the prisoners were French, the rest were Belgian, British, or American. There were others: Major Henri Fraser, François Garel, Emile Henri Garry, Pierre Culioli and a couple of Canadians - Captain John McAlister and Captain Frank Pickersgill who was in a very bad physical state. He had been wounded four times while trying to escape from a German prison in Paris. He had attacked a guard with a broken bottle and jumped from a second floor window. While running, he was hit four times by machine gun fire. Also in the carriage were Harry Peuleve and Philipp Liewer - who Benoist had met in London. Lts Marcel Leccia, Elisee Allard, Pierre Geelen, Captain Pierre Mulsant, Flying Officer Dennis Barret, and Captain Gerald Keun. Benoist was handcuffed to the American, George Wilkinson, who had been parachuted into France in May 1944 - weeks before D Day. Hessel survived the war and later he reported that the guards kept moving up and down the trucks to make sure none of the prisoners were up to any tricks, otherwise they were left alone in that dank, dark stinking carriage.

While we were racing ahead of the train, more and more ambulances had been arriving and delivering injured soldiers. They had not been in a hurry to leave the station until dusk fell, in the hope the dark would protect them. Finally the train pulled out of Gare de L'Est and worked its way out of the city through Pantin, Noisy, Bondy and Raincy to reach the river Marne. It headed out over the old WW1 battlefields. It was impossible for the prisoners to rest with the train continuously stopping and starting. Yves Loison tried endlessly to pick the lock on his handcuffs and the only discussion was if Loison managed to do it should they make a run for it. By dawn the train had not even got as far as

164

Epernay in the Champagne hills. The heat and no water made it very difficult, and the guards were growing more and more agitated as the flat land towards Chalon sur Marne. (Now Chalon en Champahe) loomed up ahead. That day an air raid had been planned on the Mercedes Benz factory at Sindlefingen near Stuttgart - amongst others. The US Eighth Air Force headed for the targets but hit bad weather, and many had to turn back with their fighter escorts. In addition there were more than 100 P47's escorted by P51 Mustangs attacking communication targets, anywhere they found them.

On this afternoon, some P47's spotted the train and attacked. The train came to a sudden stop while the drivers and guards ran away. The prisoners knew they were under attack and could hear the anti-aircraft firing with committed intent. During this period, the prisoners were able to transfer water from the lavatory into a container and pass it round to each other. Once the raid was over, the guards took their time in returning to their charge. The train was too damaged to continue and once the Germans had dealt with their own injured - sending them away by truck, they turned up with two more trucks to load the exhausted prisoners onto. This was thirty hours after they had departed from Paris. We were so close to them, if it had not been for the air raid, we would probably have not caught up with them at all. From a distance we saw the trucks leave with our objective. They were taken to the Gestapo HQ in the centre of Chalon. We arrived in Chalon just after they had left. We were told that in the confusion of the guards being given their orders, the prisoners had been allowed to wash in the town centre fountain. A few of the prisoner had been briefly able to talk with some of the locals and had given them messages in the hope they would pass some information on to their families.

The Germans were following Route Nationale 3 to

Verdun. We followed, travelling overnight to witness them leaving Verdun in the morning, heading towards the German border. I felt we had failed again but we were flogged to the degree of collapsing. We had to rest knowing we potentially had missed another opportunity to free our people. There was just never any time to re-group our thoughts, find some weapons or create a plan. We just had to follow again and again, without thought, just relentlessly travel until we were given that one chance, and then we were bloody well going to have to seize it. As we headed through Metz, people were beginning to realise the war was almost over and were showing greater signs of hostility to the Germans. This gave us hope and we started to acquire some help in small amounts. Food, water, and small arms seemed to appear from nowhere for us. They seemed to know our intent; even fresh horses were produced to allow us travel cross country. We crossed the border even more warily and found the prison camp they had been taken to. KZ Neue Bremm was situated close to Saarbrucken, it was an SS run transit camp and was an evil looking place, the like I had never imagined could exist. We found a vantage point and dug in, we were all in awe of the watchtowers and nine-foot high fences topped with electrified barbed wire. The women had been separated off and taken to another camp. I believe they were taken to Ravensbruck in the forests north of Berlin.

As the men were unloaded into the camp, they were beaten and kicked by the SS guards. I watched through my binoculars and cried. How the hell were we going to be able to affect a rescue now? This was a real con-centration camp. We were able to see the prisoners now being chained by the ankle to each other in groups of five or six. To go to the latrine they shuffled along and if one of them stumbled the SS guards immediately beat them again and again. It was unbelievably vicious. The special prisoners - my men were chained in pairs

166

and were taken to a hut behind the kitchen not more than ten by ten feet. It had one tiny window and we were able to see nothing. It must have been hell. Midsummer, hot, no room and no ventilation. Occasionally they were brought out, only to witness beatings and then put back in. After three days, we still had no plan. The prisoners were brought out, loaded on to trucks again and taken to Saarbrucken station, I thought we had lost them. Erich stepped in and with his ability to speak German, obtained more information. This train was going to the city of Weimar and that would take less than one day. We pushed on as hard as we could, it took us three days. God knows what had been happening to our boys during this period. We followed the railway lines looking for sidings, runoffs and spurs that would seem not to have heavy traffic. One lead us north of the city and we could see special fences around the end of this spur line. The camp was called KZ Buchenwald, it was here that medical experiments were being held on human beings.

When we arrived and found a safe place to dig in, we saw a group of prisoners arrive. I could only presume Uncle Robert was in there. The prisoners of war were stripped and shaved in the open, and then sprayed with chemicals, and dipped like sheep. We could smell how strong the stuff was from three quarters of a mile away. There were 13 guard towers, with nine feet fences, topped with electrified barbered wire again. The prisoners here wore uniforms that we could see were differentiated by two markings, a red triangle which we later found out was for political prisoners and yellow for Jewish. All were slave laboured for next to no rations. There were strange buildings producing a lot of smoke, which we assumed were some sort of power producing stations, but there were no power lines leaving the camp and no fuel dumps. We had heard stories but could not believe that this was what we were wit-

167

nessing. Out of all the chaps we had chased in the hope
of at least freeing uncle Robert, only three survived.
This was due to a sympathetic doctor and some very
very brave Jewish prisoners. The rest of my people fell
to Hitler's Special Orders: 'No SOE agents were to
survive the war'. They were to be given 'special treatment'. This meant either to be hung by piano wire or
taken to the crematorium, gassed below it, and then
burned. No paper trail or evidence of his or her exist-
ence was to remain. We counted them in but never had
the opportunity to count them again.

Chapter 18. Homewood Bound

At this point I was passed most forms of reason, and even when the Americans came through, the four of us remained in hiding. For me, life was over. Everything I cared about was lost or so damaged it could never be revived. Erich and Stuart had a long hard talk with me as we slowly made our way back toward Montreux. Erich drilled into me saying, "If I led them, they would work with me, not to avenge what we witnessed, but to help real people wherever we could and stop any organisation or tyrant doing what Hitler and the Nazi's had tried to do. In other words FIGHT FOR LIBERTY!" I took it all in slowly and started to think - forming a plan in my mind. As we made our way back to Switzerland, we witnessed several people who just stood out slightly, whether it was that they had been too well fed, or that their mannerisms were bullish toward others. It may have just been confidence, or having too much, then it dawned on us one at a time. These were bloody German SS men on the run to Switzerland to hide. Well I can tell you now, they weren't going to get passed us.

Once we worked out how to spot them, it became really quite easy to see who they were. I know much later, when searches were going on in the fifties and sixties, they had much more trouble finding them. Time changes people, as does the environment they are in, but for us it was not so bad, they could disguise themselves all they wanted, but they couldn't hide several things when on the road. Arrogance always shows through - even in the defeated. These monsters thought they were going to get away with their actions, as well as the goods stolen from prisoners. They carried too much weight and walked too loosely and without pain. Their skin was full, not gaunt. Generally they were cleaner and did not stink like those who had not bathed for months. They would always skulk away from uniformed allied personnel and troops. Refugees, when they saw any allied personnel, headed for them looking for news of what was happening, for food and anything they may be on offer. These German SS guys did exactly the opposite. We started to watch from a distance - not too far from Strasbourg in France which was a main thoroughfare for people to enter Switzerland but not from Germany. Obviously, the ones who had travelled this far and survived, must speak pretty fluent French, as well as their native tongue. We were interested to see what they carried with them. They seemed to always be well provisioned and able to buy whatever they wanted. We were living off the land with very little, they looked pretty well fed, so it was time to have a root around at a few.

The first one we took to one side played all the usual games, but once he realised we were acting on our own, things started to change a little. There would be no trial, no Geneva Convention to rely on, and let's face it, we had seen enough of their methods. One of the early ones we caught Stuart recognised from the last camp we had been watching, as one of the German SS Officers. He quickly admitted he had been an officer there but was only following orders. He thought he had been lucky to escape before the Americans had arrived. He thought wrong! I still had not calmed down and shamefully took it out on him. There was not much left of him by the time I'd finished. He was never going to feel fresh air inflate his lungs again. However we did learn the following:
Part of the jewellery taken from prisoners' belongings, and teeth etc, had remained on campus by order of the commandants. When the SS camp staff went on the run, they had split it between each other to help with a new start in life wherever they were running too. We had no idea how many of these men were doing this and from how many camps. What I did know was we

170

could catch a lot of them that would otherwise slip through the net, then humiliate them, and then decide what to do with the acquired precious metals and jewellery. The boys agreed it could do no harm and if it were therapeutic for me, so much the better.

We followed a pretty simple method of operation. If you looked too good, then you probably were. We only looked for individuals or pairs, just in case they were armed. We probably did let a few through the net if we were not absolutely convinced of who their former employer was. However, when we were convinced, we took no prisoners. We led them away from the road, into the local hills for a little chat. We stripped them naked - if it was raining, all the better. We would then go through their belongings, bags, suitcases - you name it, we destroyed it. This was followed by all their clothing. While we were doing this, we found copious amounts of diamonds, gold, gemstones and silver. We then held these prisoners for the few days while we worked the area. Before we moved on to avoid difficulties with the authorities, we left them in groups tied up with no clothes. We left notes around them explaining that they were ex SS troops or officers and that freedom fighters for the Resistance had secured them. I don't think we were ever going to be chased down for these thefts, but it was better to try and leave it as clean as possible. We carried on doing this for quite a while, then headed towards Dole as the amount we had acquired was becoming alarmingly large.

It took us eight days to return to Charles with our load. He happily put us up in our usual hide out while we decided what to do next. Everything was smelted down and separated into small manageable amounts. Each amount was to be just about enough for a person who was frugal to get a start in life. We then went out distributing these 'packages' to refugees who we could be pretty certain were genuine. I do still hope that these people actually did have another chance in life and were able to dismiss at least a few horrors from their minds.

I have always tried to be the best of the best, and fair and straight at all times.

Chapter 19. Return

May 29th, 1945. The bells had rang out at St Pierre
church in Neuilly-sur-Seine. The memorial service was
for Robert Benoist. Many of his racing colleagues were
able to attend and obviously some sadly were not. They
were there to honour the sacrifice Robert had made for
a free world. There was even a discreet wreath from the
British Embassy and a group of people from the consu-
late I was told. For many, it was an unpleasant surprise
to see Robert's brother Maurice present, he defended
himself enthusiastically against the rumours he had
worked with the Germans, but I do not know as I had
not been involved.

Erich and Stuart headed back to Montreux in early August. We all thought we had done enough by then. We
had agreed that once my debriefing with Vera Atkins
(and probably Buckmaster) of the SOE was over, I
would de-mobilise myself and find a new career. This
would safeguard all of us, as I had been off 'Piste' for
so long I could not know what may happen on my return to the UK. The intention was that Albert would
stay in Dole at the Monastery with Charles, after he had
returned to Evington in the U.K. to be demobilised. It
meant there was an excuse to thank again W.C. Jack
Butler, letting him know I had found Albert, and we
had some ideas for the future. All of the monies we had
not been able to distribute would be held by Charles
(who we now started to call Cash as his full name was
actually Charles Andre Stuart Hobson) for use in the
future and as a pension. None of us really knew what
the world had in store for us, we agreed to meet again
in two years' time at the Monastery with Charles.

Albert and I were in transit on our way through Paris,
heading to the UK when we heard about the race Cup
de la Resistance. We were so excited, we stayed in Par-

173

is in the hope that I may see old friends and be involved
with the fun to be held on September 15th, 1945. Those
who were from the pre-war racing world wanted to
honour Uncle Robert. Maurice Mestivier - president of
the 'Association General Automobiles des Couriers
Independents' had started planning this race meeting to
take place as soon as the War was over in Europe. It
was decided that a race would be good for morale, especially if it were held in Paris, as thousands of people
would be able to attend. Mestivier had been a mechanic
in 1921 for Amilcar and then became a driver himself,
later becoming Amilcar's chief engineer. He had
worked closely with Andre Morel and had been in
competition with Benoist, selling production road cars
before the war. Maurice Mestivier had become president of the AGACI in 1937 and even with the backing of
one of the largest Resistance organisations, it was still
difficult to organise a race so soon after the war. They
had agreed that any profit from the race would go to
former prisoners of the war and war victims. The main
difficulties were not the authorities but finding racing
cars. There were no new ones, many had been hidden
away six years ago and were in a poor state of repair.
Racing tyres were near impossible to find. The easy
part was the road circuit itself. The race was to be held
in the Bois de Boulogne, the woodland park, just west
of Paris and close to the Metro station Porte Dauphine.

The Start-Finish line was set close to the boating lake at
the crossroads at Carrefour de bout-des-lacs. The pits
were on Route de Surenses, running from the crossroads to Port Dauphine. It was only a few hundred
yards from Avenue Foch - the old SD headquarters
where we had been so close and yet so far away from
helping Robert. At Port Dauphine there was a hairpin
turn that sent the drivers back into the park, running
down Allee des Fortifications along to Avenue de saint
Cloud and then round to the right until it reached the

174

junction with Chemin de Ceinture du Lac Inferieur. This hairpin there sent them back towards the pits through an extremely technical part of the track. The 600 yards here meant going through two sets of S bends with the boating lake on their left hand side. They arrived back at Carrefour du Bout-des-Lacs, which now had become a very high-speed right hand corner. It was a cracking just-under-2-mile track. Preparations for the race had been going on right through the summer.

The war in the Pacific was going in the direction the allies expected and was coming to an end -slowly. The Americans dropped the second Atomic bomb in August and the Japanese surrendered. Two weeks later the official documents were signed on USS Missouri in Tokyo Bay, this day is now known as 'Victory in Japan day'.

Seven days after that, between 90 and 200,000 spectators turned out to see the first motor race since the end of WW2. It was named the 'Coupe Robert Benoist' - a 36-lap race for cars of 750cc to 1.5 litres. Seventeen had entered including three cars tuned and prepped by Amedee Gordini for Jean Brault, Robert Cayeux and for himself. Two old Samsons were entered for Just Emile Vernet and Robert-Aime Bouchard and a pair of Riley's driven by the engineer Pierre Ferryand and Georges Brunot. Charles Deutsch the engineer had designed the DB and was to drive his DB. A Singer was entered by Jacques Savoye, and Victor Polledry entered and drove an Aston Martin, while the rest of the field was made up of an Alder, an Amilcar, a Fiat and one small Bugatti. I only knew a few of the drivers, but I knew only too well the smell of burning racing oil, and the musical notes being blown out of the car's exhausts.

Just before the first race, Ettoire Bugatti rolled up in a Bugatti Royale and everyone rushed forward to meet

175

him. With the help of the US military police and the police of Paris, the crowd was kept under control without dampening any of their enthusiasm.

In this 36-lap race, Gordini took the lead on lap one and continued to lead his teammates through the whole 62-mile race. Nobody seemed to care about the result, they just loved the spectacle, the sound and excitement of the race. When all fell silent, a lone bugler sounded out the 'Last Post'
and instantly the crowd stood for a minute's silence in memory of Robert Benoist. He had done so much for French motor racing, even more for France and again for liberty. His daughter Jacqueline Garnier was presented with a bouquet of flowers. We sat with her before the second race and cried at our loss of those especially brave gladiators of the track.

Once the tribute was over and emotions had settled down, the engines of the competitors' cars for the main race began to roar into life. The race had been named 'Coupe de la Liberation' - it was for engines from 1.5 litre to 3 litres in capacity. Out of the fifteen entrants, there were six Amil cars, one of these were driven by Mestivier. Rene Bonnet, a co-founder of DB, was in one of his own cars. Auguste Veuillet drove an MG. (He had been a motorcycle racer and later became Porsche's importer of cars to France). Polledry appeared in an Alfa Romeo 1750. This race was won by Henri Louveau with ease, in a Maserati 6CM, his was the only 3 litre car entered. We walked through the pits and I introduced Albert to the few drivers who I knew from the old days. It was so good to be in the environment I so much enjoyed and felt at home in.

Thanks to the intervention of a friend of Jean Pierre Wimille, Captain Francois Sommer (Raumond's brother), had been released from fighting against some German strong holds where he was flying P63's. Jean Pierre arrived too late to take part in the practice or qualifying race and was told he would have to start from the back of the grid. When I saw him, I ran towards him with Berty in hot pursuit. When Jean Pierre spotted me, he dropped to his knees to catch me and we both hugged and cried. At least one of my great heroes had survived. Berty and I had prepped the great Bugatti as best we could, knowing a driver was coming, but I had no idea it was the great protégé of my Uncles. After the great fuss, I filled him in on what had happened to his driving partners. We cried again and drank a toast to them. Jean Pierre then introduced himself to Berty and told us what he could of his war. We agreed that he must win the big race in Uncle Robert's Bugatti. Jean Pierre agreed and swore on his life he would! I had walked the track with Berty early that morning, and so I discussed the racing lines with him. I was proud he trusted my knowledge to instruct him in this. I then drew out on the ground where there the track was in bad condition, as it could cause tyre failure or a reduction in adhesion to the surface, resulting in a lack of acceleration or requiring earlier deceleration. He took it all in and thanked me, I must say he was fired up and ready to go. Uncle Robert had hidden away his factory type 59/50B Bugatti works car in 1939 before the Germans could steel it. It had an eight-cylinder engine producing 450-horsepower and Jean-Pierre was going to drive it and abuse it – fantastic! Sommer had qualified at the front in his Talbot - he would probably be Jean-Pierre's biggest rival, but his Talbot only produced 250 horses.

The main event also had 16 entrants, the cars were all over 3 litres capacity and the winning prize was for the trophy Coupe des Prisoners. Seven of the entrants were driving Delahaye 135S's. The drivers included the Eugene Carboud winner of the 1938 Le Mans 24hrs. The cars were pretty much out of date but most of the big name drivers of the 1930's were present. Philippe Etancelin at 49 years old was probably past his best, he was driving an Alfa Romeo 8C. Louis Gerard was driving a ten year old Maserati 8CM. Raymond Sommer had a T26 Talbot, Lago and Pierre Levegh drove a Talbot 150C. There were five Bugatti's, the T55 driven by Paul Friderich the son of Ernest the Bugatti dealer from Nice. Maurice Trintignant was 28 and hoping to make a name for himself racing in a Type 35/51, which he called 'Grandma' - it dated back to the early 1930's. His brother Louis Trintignat had originally raced it and was killed in it at the Grand Prix of Picardie during practice. At that time Maurice was 16 and the family had sold the car. He had bought it back five years later and had just started racing it, as the war broke out. He had been doing really well and was the protégée of Jean-Pierre Wimille who was becoming the big new Bugatti star of the time. During the war 'Grandma' had been hidden under a haystack in a barn in the area of Vaucluse. As soon as the War had come to an end, he had started to restore her.

Jean Pierre was the biggest star of the Coupe des Prisoners, He told me later that day he had escaped a raid on his SOE cell at Sermaise, he had then fought with the surviving members of the Turma Vengeance movement in the Dourdoin area. As Paris was liberated, he was the liaison between the Allied forces and the Resistance. Once that had all settled down, he enlisted with Forces Aeriennes Libres. After his training he joined Group de Reconnaissance 111/33 based in Cognac flying Bell P=63s on missions against heavy pockets of German Resistance around Royan.

The state of preparation was fairly poor and out of 16 entrants nine failed to finish the Coupe des Prisoners. More importantly, as the flag dropped and the cars roared away from the start line, the crowd was on its feet and the atmosphere was electric. Jean-Pierre Wimille came from the back of the grid and was ninth by the first corner. As the flag had dropped, he engaged his clutch and the great beast released all of its 450 horses delicately to the ground through protesting screaming tyres. Seesawing at the wheel, like the possessed hero he was, he sliced though the smallest of gaps and was in fourth position by the time they crossed the start line for the first time. He then pushed his way past the third and second placed car. The crowed was ecstatic as Jean-Pierre set about chasing the leader. The crowd and the commentator were in awe of the insane over taking manoeuvres Jean Pierre had been making in the big Bugatti. Now they were witnessing the car's full potential being unleashed on the unfeeling ground. The tyres slipped, slid, tore and protested as the car was bullied and pushed beyond it limits. It was only after a few laps of the circuit that he had caught the leader and started to attack. Now he seemed to steady and settle his mind, he checked his instruments for things that were not quite right. He pumped away like crazy to pressurise his fuel tank and transport the fuel to the engine. Then he just seemed to let her go in the manner her designers had hoped for. He was off after Sommer who was in the lead and nothing was going to stop him catching his prey. The ground shook under the big Bugatti as it braked hard, and then stilled as we were deafened by the ear drumming sound of the straight through exhaust attached to the big 8-cylinder engine. My knees shook with the pleasure on hearing such music. The smell of the roaring engines, the pale blue smoke puffing out of the exhaust when the throttles were closed on the over-run was just breath-taking, I suppose it was like being in heaven.

It took a several laps to catch Sommer in his Talbot, setting his car up into the bends slightly sideways to get the best drive out of the corners he was negotiating. When the big Bugatti did catch him, they were entering the double set of S bends and Sommer deliberately balked Jean-Pierre. This caused Jean-Pierre to allow a slightly larger gap to develop through the bends and Sommer was able to hold him through the rest of the lap. The next time round time Jean-Pierre had Sommer set up with a faint to the right and what looked like an out braking attempt in the big Bugatti. What he really did was make Sommer come slightly offline on his entry into the double S's. That was all Jean-Pierre needed. He stuck close to the Talbot all the way through. As they exited the S's, Sommer kept a tight line round the long right hander coming onto the start finish straight. The Bugatti sticking tight to the Talbots tail, started to slide out wider and wider as it drifted under the enormous torque of the engine. Then Jean-Pierre changed up another gear and the race was over. His Bugatti pulled away and left the Talbot like a floundering fish. They were not even in the same race anymore, the Bugatti and Jean Pierre just kept pulling away until the flag was dropped.

After the race, Jean-Pierre Wimille told reporters, "The car was extraordinary, with this car I can win other races." On the rostrum Jean-Pierre received the Coupe des Prisoners trophy and the crowd cheered and started to celebrate - wine and beer flowing everywhere. They then all fell silent as a very frail old man with a shaven head worked his way to the rostrum with the help of some stewards. He had with him a trophy, his name was Albert Fremont, he was one of the few survivors of the Buchenwald concentration camp. He was there to present the winner of Coupe des Prisoners with the trophy Coupe de Williams. The cup had been donated by Jean Boudon, an old friend of Willy and Yvonne Grover. It was presented in Uncle Willy's honour to the only man who should have had it, Jean Pierre Wimille.

After a few days the excitement had died down so Berty and I headed back to the UK. My debriefing took longer than I thought and at the end I was asked to take a job in the civilian sector by Vera. I trusted her and knew she was to be going to Europe to help search and find anything she could about her girls. Her determination was evident, and I think she felt personal guilt, not knowing what had happened to them. At the same time the S.O.E. was disbanded, I think it was forced to by other organisations within the military not being too enamoured with the success and failings of the S.O.E.

I was sent toward under a chap call I Fleming. He had been in Navy Intelligence during the war, but now was to be running a group of reporters through the Times Newspaper. At the time I had no real idea of what I was to be doing, although I was advised it was the correct thing to do, as I had all the relevant credentials and experience. Vera suggested that I would probably excel at it.

Chapter 20. Closing Down

A side note had been slipped into the back of the diary.

Dear Nick,
Do your thing.
Research - you know knowledge is everything.
Do your job now.
Love
Murtyl.

Nick sat there with his daughter in his arms. He didn't cry, he just took big deep breaths as all the information in the diary sank into his brain. Murtyl had shown him in the days they had spent together, he now realised. The clues were all there in the things she had told him and he, the bloody idiot, had never joined up the dots and put any of the information together to make one coherent line. He hoped he had not let her down, and swore to Pip his daughter that no stone would remain unturned as he proved this all to be correct. Only when the case was bullet proof would he take the finished book, article, investigation or whatever it was to be, to Mr Ron Kirk.

It was four in the morning and he made his way to bed, collapsing exhausted with Pip still in his arms.

He didn't dream, he was just gone!

This book is a work of fiction based roughly on fact. It is written in honour of the 42 very special and brave ladies who were recruited by the 'Special Operations Executive'. Sadly only eleven were to survive the war. It is also to honour all those who lived and fought through those terrible times.

Information of true historical events have been used, and are referenced as follows:
The Grand Prix Saboteurs by Joe Seward
She Landed by moonlight. by Carole Seymor-Jones
Early one morning. by Robert Ryan
The spy who loved. Claire Mulley
Outwitting the Gestapo by Lucie Aubrac
Life in secrets by Sarah Helm
Mrs Mahoney's secret war. by Gretel Mahoney and Claudia Strachan
The Bugatti Queen by Miranda Seymor
Heroines of SOE. Britain's secret women in France. F Section
Moondrop to Gascony by Anne Marie Walters.

About Dr Chris Pearson:
Dr Chris Pearson is a doctor of traditional medicines who treats private patients - both human and animal, as required. His aim is always to find a way to take a patient from a state of dis-ease and enable them to be in a state of ease. His inspiration to write this book and start the Murtyl Diaries series off, was through both his sporting knowledge and competing in pre-war racing cars around the UK. This kindled an interest in the pre-war era and the brave drivers. WW11 then stopped the world and changed it. After reading many books on the subject, he thought that the younger generation were never going to learn, know or understand what heroes their Great-Grandparents had to be. With this in mind, the following adventures are being written. He also hopes it will help young ladies gain more respect from

those around them and stand up for their rights. They are, and always will be, as good as men: Never give up, when you think all hope has left and buggered off, try again. You are all winners; you just have to know it.

As a first time writer I wish to thank the following for their patience and help:
Cpt N J Pearson
Hob
Jack
Jo
Johnny
Kevin Robinson
Lex Ruddiman
Lisa Smith
Lucinda and Cara Eggerton
Sarah Harbour
Steve Robinson.

One last thing: This book was whacked of with one finger on a keyboard by a man in Yorkshire.

Printed in Great Britain
by Amazon